TROUBLE IN TRONDHEIM

KURT HAMMER BOOK 1

MATS VEDERHUS

To:
Sjeik, a friend without words.
Line, a friend with words.
Marte, for inspiration.

PROLOGUE

In that moment, his pose told her there was no going back.

His eyes popped out of his head. They reminded her of ones she'd seen on frogs they were about to dissect in elementary school. Sticking out of his mouth was a swollen tongue. The hue of his skin had turned a sickly green. A tailor-made suit clung stiffly and lifelessly to his body, all its former glory now nothing but a vague memory.

Why did he call me a whore? It wasn't so much the word, but its associations which brought out her inner devil. Before leaving, she had promised herself that this land would mean a fresh start.

Sighing, she turned, exited the booth, and closed its door behind her. *I couldn't help it. It was his fault.* She entered the entrance hall in Værnes airport.

Outside, the rain had settled in. She got in the first taxi she could find.

"Where're you going?"

"Brothel," she replied.

1

Unsettled by the welcome, she still decided this country had potential.

———

In AFTENBLADET's new premises in the Ferjemanns road number 10, an atmosphere of controlled chaos reigned supreme. Almost all the journalists were on an assignment or worked from home while they waited for the office landscape to be completed. Editor Karlsen found his way to one of the few employees who were present among moving boxes, flat packs from IKEA, printers and laptops that were set up on makeshift surfaces.

"Hammer, you idiot, wake up. A guy was murdered in a toilet booth!"

"Hm, zzz... what?"

Looking down on his most unreliable employee was Editor-in-Chief Karlsen.

"At Værnes, to be precise. I guess I ought to let you sleep on, but there isn't anyone else around right now."

"Relax, boss. Hansen and I will take care of this."

Karlsen sighed. "That's what I was afraid you'd say. Just don't drink any more beer."

"I won't," he mumbled, grabbing his tweed coat from his chair, and haplessly put it on over his yellow suit. "Hansen, let's go. We're headed for Værnes."

The young journalist Frank Hansen looked up from his monitor, throwing a sceptic look at the tall figure. *Who was it Felicia in Culture had said he looked like? Jeff Bridges! Even with a fedora and a cigarette constantly hanging out of his mouth, there was no mistaking the comparison.*

Looks wise, they couldn't have been more different. Frank Hansen was of medium build, with slightly too much fat around his abdomen. He had short brown hair and blue eyes sitting closely together that appeared to be blinking a lot.

"Fine, but I don't drink at work, just so you know."

"That's only cos you're still new to the game, Hansen!"

"Relax, Hammer. I know what happened. Everyone knows. It made the national headlines, damn it."

Hammer snorted and didn't say anything else until they'd entered one of Aftenbladet's cars.

"Listen, you little piece of shit. That's not why I drink, just so we're clear about that. It's been two years. I'm past that by now."

"Okay. If it'd been me, I'd probably taken out early retirement and gone to the Bahamas. I think you've handled the situation well. But I still don't drink at work."

Hammer leaned into his seat and pulled his fedora down over his forehead as they sped towards Værnes.

OCTOBER 9, 2011

Everything started at Trolla Brug in Trondheim. Outside the old, rundown shipyard stood three trailers with Russian license plates. Each of them had a tail of people throwing bags containing heroin to each other in the rain.

Kurt Hammer stood on one of the trailers, relieved that five hundred kilos of heroin were soon out of the cars. Out of the shipyard walked Padda, a large, bulky bald man looking like a former strongman and a flat face, who made up one-half of the leadership in Trondheim Hells Angels.

"Lars?" Kurt looked questioningly at the bald face planted between two enormous shoulders. "You're free to go. I'll take it from here. The guys have done well. The trailers are almost empty."

"Sure?"

"Unless you want to help us split the shit into bags?"

"No, thanks. I'll pass on that, at least until tomorrow."

Kurt threw the bag in his hands to the Russian behind him, before jumping down from the trailer and onto his Triumph

Thunderbird. It originated from a police seizure, and this past month had barely seen him outdoors without it.

The drive to Ila took him all of six minutes, and three minutes later in front of the Prinsen hotel, he thought about making a detour to the police station to hand in his pistol and machine gun. But the thought of seeing his fiancé, Marte, and his newly born daughter again made him quickly ditch the idea.

He sped on past the old grey brick building with red details that was Prinsen cinema. When he passed Studentersamfundets red façade, he was bombarded with raindrops the size of golf balls. Finally, outside his flat in Volveveien 11A at Nardo, water and sweat dripped off his entire body. The four-room flat looked like a wooden square, painted white, with a small quadratic shed in front of it which also served as a storage place for garbage containers. Coupled with the first flat was another flat, this one oblong and painted black, also with its own shed in front.

He jumped off the bike and gave it a clap on its seat before walking across the gravel and putting his hand on the doorknob. Closed. Perhaps she was sleeping in?

He found the key under the mat on which he stood before, put it in the keyhole and turning the lock.

"Hello, Marte? I'm home."

No one answered. Instinctively, he went out the door again and picked up his gun from the bag on the bike. Inside, he could feel a cold breeze emanating from the kitchen. The living room window turned out to have been shattered, but beyond that, he could find no signs of anything out of the ordinary. He couldn't find any footprints. That should be impossible in this weather. *The people who had broken in must have removed their shoes.*

With his pistol still in both hands, he entered the

bedroom. At once, all doubts about the unknown perpetrator's identity faded. A stench of blood had spread out in the large, whitewashed room. In the black Fjell double bed from Ikea, Marte lay chained with two handcuffs. Her long, curly tresses wound neatly down past her shoulders. A gaping grimace had melted itself onto her face as a sort of cruel last goodbye. A bullet hole had manifested in her forehead, another in her stomach. The duvet was steeped in blood. He could barely watch the cot in the other side of the room. What was there wasn't so much the remains of a human being as a cadaver.

He turned on his heel and went back to his bike. Rationally speaking, he should've dialed 112. But rational thinking had just gone out the window.

He drove from Nardo to Trolla Brug in a blind, violent rage, with an average speed of eighty kilometers an hour. When he arrived, the trailers were already gone, but he found most of the bikes still parked outside. The last thing he did before going in was to put on the bulletproof vest placed in his bike's bag. Inside the warehouse stood Padda, Martin, Ramberg, Flisa, and several others. Some were opening bags. Others were splitting the heroin into small Ziplock bags.

If my colleagues had been here, they'd have laughed at the entire operation. How extremely careless.

However, they weren't there. It was just him and his machine gun. It turned into a real battle. Heroin and blood squirted everywhere, like paint onto the misty grey relief outside.

Half an hour later, it was all finished. Twenty or so bodies were scattered on the grey concrete floor, on wooden tables, and behind boxes. Without a word, he hoisted himself up from a crouching position, went outside, positioned himself on the bike, and drove home.

A few hours later, he turned on the television in Volveveien 11A.

"Trolla Brug has witnessed what looks to be a gang war. Trolla Brug is Hell's Angels' headquarters in Trondheim. Seventeen people were murdered and three people severely injured in what the police describe as the worst shootout in the history of Trondheim."

Kurt Hammer opened another bottle of Jack Daniels and waited for the sirens.

APRIL 27, 2010

THERE WAS A DISRUPTIVE MOOD ACROSS ALL NRK.
Fifteen minutes remained until the news of the day, *Dagsnytt*,
was going to air at 7:00 p.m., and there were rumors that an
important visitor was on his way to the newsroom. Jon Gelius
was sitting in makeup when Nina Owing entered and sat in the
chair next to him.

"Have you heard it," she whispered, as she had a little
rouge applied on her cheeks.

"No, what?"

"You're aware that Medvedev's visiting, right?"

Jon nodded. He was, of course, aware that Medvedev was
in Oslo to sign an agreement on boundaries in the Barents Sea
and Arctic Ocean. It was going to be one of the main stories in
the broadcast.

Nina continued to whisper. "I was told by the reception
that he might be on his way here."

"Are you kidding?"

"I know it sounds... far out. Just about far enough that it
might be true. What do you think?"

Jon contorted his face in deep folds. "Do you know whether Hans–Wilhelm is on duty?"

"I actually think he is." She smiled.

About fifteen minutes later, the two were presenting the broadcast in the studio. Just as the main stories had been presented, Jon received a message on the ear from producer Geir.

"Medvedev's in the reception, with an interpreter. The broadcast will be extended by ten minutes. Russia has just entered Schengen. Amazing scoop!"

Jon was perplexed for a few long seconds.

"Well, I've just heard on my ear here that… President Dmitry Medvedev is heading into the studio to talk about… Russia has become a member of Schengen."

The cameramen and script looked at each other as if they couldn't believe what they'd just heard. One minute of silence followed.

"Yeah, uh, this is taking some time." Jon swore under his breath.

Nina tried to save the situation. "Tonight's main story is that Medvedev came to Oslo to sign an agreement on the borders to the Barents Sea. Let's take a look at the story."

Just as the story started running, Medvedev came casually walking into the studio.

"I have an announcement to make." He stood right next to Jon and Nina.

"Please stand over here." Jon pointed. "Welcome!"

"Thank you." Medvedev shook his hand before moving to the place Jon had pointed out.

The cameraman began counting down. "5, 4, 3, 2…"

Jon announced, "Yes, then we have Medvedev in the studio. Mr. President, you said you had an announcement to make?"

He smiled, triumphantly. A winning smile, targeting cameras, and Jon could understand why he was president.

"Yes, today, here in Oslo, I signed an agreement between Norway and my country. But more importantly, yesterday Russia officially became a part of Schengen. This was the result of many months of intense negotiations, and I am pleased to say that Russian citizens can now travel freely without a visa, across the border to Norway. It also means that, for the first time, Norwegians can visit my beautiful city of St. Petersburg without first submitting a visa application. This is great news and I hope it will better the relations between Europe and Russia."

Nina gasped. "When will this agreement be put into effect?"

"Well, as with all such things, there is a lot of paperwork that needs to be processed, but we are currently looking at the winter of 2011."

"That's great! Did you have any other motivation besides promoting tourism?"

"Yes, we are hoping, as I said, to promote our relations with Europe in general, and our trade relations in particular."

"Are you trying to compete with Norway's oil and gas exportations," asked Jon.

Medvedev smiled, bashfully this time. "Well, Russia has traditionally had its own markets, including Ukraine in particular. But that is part of it, yes."

"Did you discuss this with Jens Stoltenberg?"

"Actually, no. You guys are the first to hear. Jens is such a nice man. There was no need to upset him with such details."

"Aren't you afraid he's going to feel... cheated?"

"Absolutely not! He will find out at the same time as everyone else."

"Well, we have to move on now," Jon said. "But thanks for coming here to share this important news."

"The pleasure was all mine."

Medvedev left his assigned place, and just as Nina was going to present the next story, he came over and kissed her on the cheek before leaving as abruptly as he had arrived. A collective gasp went through the studio as blonde Nina turned red as a tomato.

JANUARY 26, 2012

Olya's mother died suddenly. After her coffin was lowered into the earth and the families had departed, Olya was left to herself when she got home.

In her heart, she knew he would come home, as he'd done countless times before. When she heard the front door being opened just after midnight, it presented itself as something of a bad dream.

"Olya, are you at home?!"

She lay with her eyes closed and hoped he wouldn't come into the room. *Was the door locked, was the door locked, was the door locked...*

"Why don't you answer, you cheeky little piece of shit?"

She opened one eye and peered out from the edge of her quilt. He reeked of Stolichnaya.

"You're drunk, Papi. Go and lie down."

"What, are you talking back to your papi? You fucking whore!"

He tore off her quilt, lifted her up by the scruff and threw her into the wall.

13

"It's your fault that she's dead, you know? She had heart trouble from taking care of you, you ungrateful—"

She gathered what little strength she had and headbutted him. He staggered a bit before falling hard. She ran as fast as she could through the hallway, into the kitchen, and tore up the nearest kitchen drawer. Panic stricken, she grabbed a bread knife. Then she heard him come into the kitchen. With the knife in both hands, she turned to face him, wide-eyed with her body shaking like a leaf. "What are you going to do?" he sneered. "Come and take me."

Unable to move, she could only remain frozen and watch him approach with unsteady steps on the tattered kitchen rug. Finally, his face was less than a meter from hers.

The next thing that happened should be seen in light of her mother's bruised and swollen eyes. Anyone who saw her knew, but no one said anything, not even at the funeral. All the years of beating, name-calling, and shit-stirring were discharged at the moment she drove the knife into him.

A few seconds of silence followed before he whispered, "Help me, Olya, help me!"

Her thoughts disappeared back to her mother again. She saw her lying in a pool of her own blood, in the morning, while he slept in in their bedroom. Her beautiful golden hair was sticky and disgusting. Olya had to help her into the bathroom, undress her, shower her, and massage her. All without saying a word.

Silence said more than any of us could have formulated by opening our mouths.

Her five-year-old self went around him. Her twenty-year-old self pulled up the carpet before closing the door behind her.

———

AMONG MOSCOW's population is whispered a proverb. *Man has not felt cold on his body before he has experienced winter in Moscow.*

Midway between several meter-high snow banks on either side of Tverskaya Street, Olya was now facing what amounted to miles of shop facades. A few meters beyond the block she lived in, some of them were still open even though it was thirty below. On a stand, she noticed a newspaper front page with a picture of Putin and his wife. At the top read *Divorce,* in screaming letterheads. She picked up a copy of a paper and went into the little grocery store behind the stand.

"Olga, right?"

She nodded meekly to the bearded giant behind the counter, showed him the newspaper, and left a ruble in front of him.

"Condolences! Greet your papi, from Oleg. He must be absolutely horrified now."

She smiled, and muttered, "Thank you, I will," before turning to leave.

Right before she closed the door, she stopped. *How had he looked at me, the old pig?* She tore off a piece of newsprint and wrote down her address. Then she paused for a few seconds, before adding, *thirty minutes.* Finally, she went back in, handed him the note, and disappeared again without saying a word.

Back in the apartment, she opened the kitchen window onto the side street, and aimed at a garbage container she had opened. She gathered what strength she had once more, eased her father's body onto the kitchen counter, and pushed it out the window. The fall from the twenty-second floor was spectacular. If he wasn't already dead, he was guaranteed to be, as he landed headfirst far below. She let out an involuntary shout of joy as she became filled with relief, because when someone found the now dismembered body below, she would be far away.

Soon, a knock came at the front door. No matter how much it filled her with disgust, she forced herself to down a glass of Stolichnaya before she went to open it. In the hallway, she walked past a mirror. The dark curls she had from her father were bursting in all directions, but there was nothing she could do about it right now. Her verdigris almond eyes were her best feature, so she took a little eyeliner from the dresser and put it on before applying a coat of lipstick to her voluptuous lips. The red matched her hair and eyes.

"You're one-fourth Spanish," her mother had said one day, after Olya came home from school.

Somehow, she had always known it.

"My papi was Spanish," her mother had said, with a smile and winked at her.

She'd never mentioned him before, but it explained the golden color of their skin. The night had been particularly hard, which was probably the reason she had mentioned him then.

"Did he die before I was born?"

"He probably did. He lived in Málaga, you see. My mami brought me here just after I was born. She was homesick but never forgot about papi. Come." Her mother pulled Olya into their bedroom, then sat on the bed and patted beside her. "Here." She handed her daughter a faded picture from her wallet.

To the left of her mother stood a man with almond eyes, a nose that was too big for his face, and a charming smile parked in the middle of a forest of a beard. He wore a sailor's cap, slightly askew.

"He could've been my papi," said Olya.

They smiled at each other for the first time in a long while.

With the image of her grandpa fresh in mind, she went and opened the front door.

Oleg was even larger than she remembered. Before he could open his mouth, she blurted an insane sum. He opened his wallet, gave her cash, and stepped over the threshold.

A few hours later, she stood in one of the counters at Sheremetyevo airport.

"Do you have a ticket to Malaga for nine thousand rubles?"

"Hmm. Not until the end of next month, at least."

Well, you can get to Trondheim, Norway in a few hours, for eight thousand."

She thought about it. *Norway is a rich country, isn't it?* Her papi had said so. He'd been fishing there with a buddy. Apparently, they had really big salmon, too.

"All right, she finally said. I'm going to Norway."

SHOT IN SELF-DEFENSE

BY HARRY OLSEN AND HANNE ESTENSTAD

Former NCIS employee Kurt Hammer was declared innocent of premeditated murder today by Frostating Court. However, he has lost his job due to gross negligence in the service.

None of the surviving Hell's Angels members have wanted to testify about the drama that unfolded in the former shipyard Trolla Brug on March 21st. Thus, the Court of Appeal found no grounds for the prosecution's claim that Kurt Hammer deliberately killed those present.

Hammer is linked to the crime scene by DNA evidence, but has always maintained that he shot in self-defense.

"This ruling is sensational and will set a precedent for similar cases," was Prosecutor Inga Bejer Engh's brief comment to Aftenbladet after the trial.

A clearly affected Kurt Hammer was very relieved. "Now, I'm going home to Nardo and will try to put this behind me. This verdict shows that there is a functioning court system in Norway," he said, before he disappeared into a waiting car with his attorney Harald Stabell.

Hammer lost his fiancée and newborn daughter on the same

day as the shooting incident, and the case is still under investigation.

Gross Negligence

Previously, it has been known that Hammer was ordered to resign from his position in the NCIS due to what the Norwegian Bureau for the Investigation of Police Affairs describes as "gross negligence in service." Hammer has not appealed the decision.

Gigantic Seizure

Aftenbladet has learned that Hammer was at Trolla Brug undercover. Here, he was to help take down the people behind the smuggling of five hundred kilos of heroin, the largest seizure ever in Norway.

"We don't know exactly who is behind this, but we are working closely with law enforcement and know that it revolves around a group of traffickers from Russia who have collaborated with Hell's Angels in Trondheim. When it concerns an amount sufficient enough to supply all of Trondheim for a year, we are extremely worried about how they intended to distribute this and who they intended to sell to," said Vidar Hanevold, of the Department for Organized Crime, division of the Trondheim Police.

JANUARY 28, 2012

"Let me past!"

"No one slips past police checkpoints. Especially not you, Hammer!"

Inspector Roy Dundre curled his thin lips into an oily smile. His small, brown eyes exuded a superiority many times larger than their actual size. Next to Hammer, he resembled a dwarf but wouldn't let himself be pushed around.

"You idiot," Hammer said. "You know that I won't destroy evidence."

"It doesn't matter!"

Frank Hansen gripped his older colleague's shoulder and dragged him away.

"Quiet now, Hammer. Can't you go and have a coffee so I can take a picture and at least get some background information?"

Hammer said nothing but turned resolutely on his heels and disappeared in the direction of Starbucks. Hansen let out a sigh of relief and turned his camera lens towards the sealed body within the boundary of the white and red police tape.

"What do you really know about the deceased?" he asked.

"Christian Blekstad," Dundre replied, "thirty-seven years of age, worked for Adnor Lawyers in Dronningensgate. He'd been on a business trip to Moscow. They wouldn't say what he was doing there. But could I please ask for some discretion. We haven't yet informed the family."

Hansen smiled. "Of course. We can wait to publish online till you've talked to 'em. If you could call me ..." He pulled out his card, said thanks, and went to Hammer.

"Hm?"

"Lawyer and family man, went by the name of Christian Blekstad. Worked for Adnor Lawyers. Police haven't informed the family yet, so we have to wait with posting personal information online."

"Hmm." Hammer looked down at his Grande Latte Macchiato for a moment. "Do you have any theories?"

"Honestly, no."

"Well, I do."

Hansen looked at him, questioningly.

"Experience, Hansen, experience. Most likely done by someone from abroad. Why the hell would anyone go out here to whack him? I also think it was a man, simply because it was done in the men's room."

"Well, you're the one who'll be writing the text, not me."

"Do I detect a hint of skepticism in your voice?"

"Well, if someone had a really good motive, economically, for example."

Hammer sighed.

"If there's one thing I learned from my time in NCIS, it is that one should look at opportunity first and foremost. That immediately reduces the list of suspects."

Frank looked at Kurt. "As long as there's a good story."

Kurt Hammer got up from his bed in room 324 at the Prinsen hotel, to the sound of knocks on the door. When he opened it, he was greeted by a girl he didn't think could be more than twenty years old. She was wearing a floor-length sequin silver dress which complimented her golden skin. Her dark curls swung from side to side as she strode across the threshold and pushed him down onto the bed.

"Boxers off," she commanded.

"*Nyet*," he replied. Massage."

She was silent.

"I have been with many men in many places, but none have ever told me not to have sex with them."

"I'm not like any other man you've met. Trust me."

Fifteen minutes earlier, he had walked into the shower. *You old fool, Hammer. You're thirty-seven. What the hell are you doing!*

For a moment, he considered sending her a text to cancel, but his year-long self-imposed celibacy was about to expire. Though, Marte still haunted his dreams both day and night.

He got out of the shower. *She wouldn't have wanted me to become a criminal.*

Just as Lola Bunny's long, strong fingers drilled down into the upper part of his back, he tried to imagine that she was Marte.

"Why Lola Bunny?"

"Shh."

He let out a deep groan. *No more stupid attempts at talks.* He had longed for this.

DEAD LAWYER FOUND AT VÆRNES

BY KURT HAMMER AND FRANK HANSEN

Early in the morning on January 27th, a corpse was discovered at the airport, by a cleaning lady. The deceased's identity has been confirmed by local police.

Lawyer Christian Blekstad, thirty-seven years old, had just arrived from Moscow on a mission for the Adnor Lawyers firm, of which he was a partner. Police investigators are theorizing that he was drowned.

"It was absolutely terrible! How's it possible for anyone to bring themselves to do such a thing?" said cleaning lady Agnieszka Pavlova.

Confidential

Partner and lawyer with Adnor Lawyers, Tore Hallan, confirmed that the deceased had been in Moscow, but wouldn't say why.

"No, that's confidential. I can reveal that I would be very surprised if it had something to do with anything that could be a potential motive for murder."

Hallan said to Aftenbladet, that all employees at Adnor

Lawyers are in shock after the news, and that their thoughts go out to his family. The firm has already contacted their clients to agree on a day off during the week.

Aftenbladet has been in contact with Blekstad's widow, who has told her lawyer that she would prefer to be left alone with her children during this difficult period. She is happy for all the support and warm thoughts.

JANUARY 29, 2012: MORNING

Olya was situated in front of a three-floored fixer on Byåsen. Across the road was a stop on Gråkallbanen line, the northernmost tram line in the world. She couldn't rid herself of the thought of how ironic it was that she had had to go all the way to Norway to discover it.

The rain splashed down, but her hair was as curly as ever even though she was soaked as she stood outside a building covered in flaking brown paint. She wore a beige trench coat and high-heeled red shoes with sequins. The garden outside looked as if it had just been mowed, and was surrounded by a well-groomed hedge that stood in stark contrast to the old house.

She rang the bell in front of a white door next to a small note labeled *Jansrud*. The door was opened by a tall, handsome man with an athletic physique.

He peered at her with his narrow blue eyes. "Lola Bunny?"

She nodded.

"Petter. Come in."

She went in and hung her outerwear in a narrow hall

covered with wood paneling. Straight ahead, it led to a kitchen overlooking the garden. To the right, it was connected by a staircase leading to the upper floors.

———

KURT HAMMER WOKE ABRUPTLY, inside the toilet outside Trondheim Torg shopping center, from what felt like a rain shower. He rubbed his eyes and realized that the automatic washing mechanism was to blame. He opened the door to the sound of raindrops, with only a bottle of Stolichnaya left inside the booth.

"Damn, Hammer. When will you learn that drinking causes headache," he said to himself.

He entered the McDonalds restaurant next to the toilet, with fragments of the previous night still on his retina. Glanced at his Omega wristwatch, a Planet Ocean 600m, which he'd received from Marte when they got engaged, and noted that it was already ten o'clock. Out of habit, he ordered a double cheeseburger before he sat to wait for a taxi.

Five hours later, he woke up at home in Volveveien, to the sound of his cell phone ringing on the bedside table.

"Hammer, speaking."

It was Hansen. "Hammer, we've been asked to write a portrait of Petter Jansrud. We're supposed to meet him at his home in about an hour."

Hammer let out a long sigh.

"It struck me that you might've forgotten about it."

"Relax, I've already written all the questions."

"What a relief. Shall I pick you up?"

"No, I'll meet you there!"

He hung up, confirmed that his damned headache was about to let go, and hauled himself out of bed. Outside the bathroom, he looked in the mirror, and despite that the previous evening was something of a mystery, he didn't look too bad. The stubble on his chin was two-days old. It could wait another day. The long hair that reached his shoulders was greasy, but he had no time for a shower now. His narrow blue eyes looked pale and tired, but that could be fixed.

In the outer corridors, he donned a brown leather jacket over his canary yellow suit. He picked up a pair of Ray Ban Aviators from the inside pocket and put on his bucket helmet with a white skull logo on it. Outside, he sat on his Harley Davidson EL Knucklehead, purchased with Marte's life insurance, and left Volveveien 11A with a roar.

About twenty minutes later, he drove past Ilaparken, which lay deserted in the rain, with its music pavilion and its playground. The day before Marte died, they'd been sitting on the benches, looking at children who climbed the racks and swung on the swings.

"In a few years, we can bring her here," she said, with a smile.

"Maybe we should move to Ila," he said, returning her smile.

She put her head onto his shoulder as a tacit confirmation.

Five minutes later, he rolled up next to a brown house with three floors on Byåsen, and parked the bike in the gravel driveway. As he dismounted, the Gråkallbanen train passed in the direction of Ila. Its tracks lay barely fifty meters from the house. Hammer realized that he was a little early, but thought it couldn't hurt to call.

He called once. No answer.

Again. Still no answer.

He touched the door knob. The door was open.

Petter wouldn't want me to stand in the rain. He walked into a narrow corridor covered with wood paneling which led into a kitchen overlooking the garden.

"Hello?"

No answer.

Just then, he heard a car driving into the driveway. He decided to ignore it. He took off his shoes and walked up the white wooden staircase to the right. The first floor smelled of paint and mineral spirits. Two doors were open to a room filled with paint cans, wallpaper rolls, and flat packages from IKEA.

"Kurt?" Hansen's voice yelled, from the ground floor.

"I'm up here," Hammer said, curtly, as he continued up the stairs.

The top floor had a large living room with windows that provided views across Trondheim. On the front banister was a burgundy leather couch in front of a forty-eight-inch TV.

"Hansen, I think you should come up."

At the other end of the room was the muscular body of cross-country skier Petter Jansrud, clamped in leather straps connected to a rope attached to the two side walls. His clothes lay in a heap on the wooden floor, and his erect limb was cut off and placed in his mouth.

"What is it," Hansen asked, from behind Kurt.

Hammer lit a Prince Rounded Taste cigarette and blew a long streak of smoke into the room.

"Hansen, I think we have a murder case on our hands."

JANUARY 29, 2012: DAY

"Should I call—"

"Don't even think about it," Hammer said. "Take pictures first."

Hansen circled the body from every angle while the flash lamp went off like a machine gun.

"I don't know how many of those we can use." He sighed. "The poor man is shredded."

He picked up his cell phone from his jacket pocket as Kurt Hammer lit another cigarette.

A mere fifteen minutes later, as the two men sat on the burgundy sofa and looked out at Trondheim city, they were enlightened by shades of red and blue. Crime Inspector Roy Dundre was first up the stairs. His face was flabby and it turned a bright shade of blue when he was stressed. Once he turned and saw the corpse, he collapsed to his knees and remained there for a few seconds.

As an army of technicians in white coats came up the stairwell, he turned to Hammer and Hansen and barked, "You two, to the station with me. Pronto!"

"Calm down," Hammer said, calmly. "We know the routines. Can we drive ourselves, or will you get someone to pick up our car and bike?"

———

WHILE SITTING in a police car and peering at the rain, which seemed to wash away everything outside, Kurt Hammer conjured up some thoughts on what to say during the interview. Depending on how long Jansrud had been dead, it would seem random or mildly suspicious that the two had appeared and found the interviewee hung up with his own penis in his mouth. *Why in the name of fuck didn't I tape the interview agreement?* He cursed himself for being in the wrong place at the wrong time.

Before he had time to arrive at some reasonable explanation other than the obvious, the police car turned a corner beside the bombastic police building built from green metallic and gray concrete. Kurt looked longingly out the window at Trondheim Central Station and wished he could get on a train with a crate of lager.

Interrogation room two. He had been here a few times before everything went wrong. He remembered drawings of old wooden walls, the big curtain-covered mirrors behind the round interrogation table, and soft carpet. He even remembered that this was the biggest room, yet apparently not designed for more than one person. Therefore, he withdrew a chair from the oblong table in the corner and let Hansen sit down on the chair that was already by the interrogation table.

Roy Dundre glanced at the clock in one corner, which switched between showing the time and date. He sat, and pressed on the pedal under the table to start recording.

"The current time is 11:58 a.m. The date is the 29th of

January. Crime Inspector Roy Dundre has journalist Kurt Hammer and photographer Frank Hansen in for questioning, in connection with the murder of Petter Jansrud. The deceased was found by Hammer, in his house on Byåsen, whereupon Hansen quickly emerged." Then he blew himself up before he continued. "Any particular reason why the two of you found yourselves on the spot where one of Norway's biggest sports stars was shredded?" He leaned over the table and stared from Hansen to Hammer.

"We'd agreed to an interview. Easy. I phoned him up, but got no answer and found that the door was open."

"And you?"

"I showed up a few minutes later and saw that the door was open. Kurt had already gone inside."

"Do you have an alibi?" he asked Hansen.

"Talk with Felicia at the entertainment desk. She can confirm that I was on duty."

"I lay home and slept," said Hammer "I was seen at Cafe Dublin yesterday and McDonalds this morning. If you think I had any reason to whack him, you can arrest me."

The door to the interrogation room opened and a young police officer stepped inside.

"Dundre, there's a call waiting for you."

"Can't you see I'm busy," he snapped.

The officer came over and whispered something in Dundre's ear before he left.

Dundre coughed. "Excuse me for a moment." Then he disappeared out the door.

Hansen stared blankly at his colleague. "What was that?"

"No idea."

A little later, Dundre came back again, with his eyes fixed on the floor. When he raised his head, both of them could see that his face had turned deathly pale.

"You... you didn't notice anything unusual about the bicycle when you were driving," he said to Hammer.

"No?"

"The bicycle exploded right by Trondheim Torg. Fortunately, no other vehicles were damaged, but we lost a colleague who had just graduated. He had just become engaged."

All three were silent for a few seconds, before Edith Piaf broke the silence by calling Hammer's cell phone. He took it out of his jacket pocket and stared blankly at it for a few moments before standing up.

"Excuse me, can I take this? It's from the desk."

Dundre nodded. Frank put the cell to his ear and started circling around the room because he was unsure if it would be acceptable to go out.

"Hi. Yes, it was with us. He was dead. We're at the station now. Yes, do it! Bye."

Hammer turned toward Dundre. "Can we go?"

Dundre gave him a bewildered stare. "Yes, of course, but... eh, do you think you need protection, Kurt?"

"I'll manage. But thanks for the offer."

"Yes, but I'm going to send you to the editors in a car at the very least, for safety's sake."

———

In AFTENBLADET's newly built newsroom on Solsiden, editor Harry Karlsen had already booked a conference room with Acting Head of Desk, Felicia. Her icy blue eyes and bright red lips on a perfectly shaped fifty-five-kilo body contrasted Karlsen's clean-shaven head on a 77-inch high and one hundred fifty kilo heavy body dressed in a tailored gray suit.

"So?" Hammer said.

He, Hansen, and Karlsen sat around a glass table, while

Felicia took down the window fitting shrouds to block out the sound of rain against the big window surfaces that constituted one long wall. She sat beside him and waved her hand to remove the smoke from Karlsen's Cuban.

"So you were going to interview one of the largest athletes in Norway," Karlsen said, "and ended up at an interrogation in Gryta?"

"He was already dead as could be when I showed up," Hammer said.

"And you, Hansen. I reckon you took pictures?"

"Of course. But if you envisioned front-page news, I hardly think they can be used. The guy was... well, let me just say that police technicians got a lot of work ahead of them."

"Of course I envisioned front-page news," Karlson barked. "Kurt, go and talk to the online manager immediately. She's working on a story that'll be in the paper tomorrow. Felicia, get the sport desk to make a comment and an obituary with lots of pictures." He used his cigar to point at Hansen. "And you, concentrate on finding pictures to go with the story."

———

THE MOST OBVIOUS feature of Hanne Estenstad's office, besides large windows overlooking the Nidelven river, was the large flat screen televisions along one short wall. They showed a continuous update of the content on Aftenbladet.no. Kurt Hammer didn't notice any of the TVs when he entered, even though he knew they were there.

He nonchalantly sank into the black designer chair on the other side of an enormous workbench, and tried to picture Hanne as a bottle of Jack Daniels, in his mind's eye.

"You were going to do a portrait, weren't you?" asked Hanne.

Hammer smiled. "You can say I wasn't fully prepared."

"What, you've never experienced anything like this in NCIS?"

"Wait until you see the pictures, Hanne. I'm guessing they'll have to be censored. Otherwise, you'll have to get the graphics desk to come up with an illustration."

The sound of rain against the window panes was competing, against the sound of Hanne's fingers tapping the keyboard in front of her, for the dubious honor of making him mad, faster.

"Oh, well," she said. "Have you been checked out of the case? What did they ask about at the police station?"

"Not officially, no. But we were free go when it became clear that my bike exploded at Trondheim Torg, with a policeman on top. I believe they understood that I couldn't have been responsible for both."

The illusion of the Jack Daniels bottle was broken when her chubby little face and blond curls turned almost as white as the teeth covered by her red lips.

"Lord. Was that you! Sorry, Kurt, I had no idea."

Silence.

"Neither did I. I think Dundre, the detective inspector, must've understood how shocked I was. He actually offered me protection, but I said I didn't need it."

She gaped. "Does that mean that someone's looking for you? Do you think it might be connected to the murders?"

"I have no idea, Hanne. But so far... right now I'm just happy to be alive."

CROSS-COUNTRY SKIER FOUND DEAD

BY KURT HAMMER

Aftenbladet can confirm that cross-country skier Petter Jansrud was found dead in his house, in Byåsen. It was Aftenbladet's journalist Kurt Hammer who discovered the deceased in what should have been a portrait in the Sunday edition.

"As a former NCIS employee and journalist, I have seen many things, but this was shocking even to me," Hammer said to Aftenbladet.

Jansrud was found strapped from the walls of the upper floor of the house. Police have no suspects or motive in the case.

Absolutely Unreal

"This is absolutely unreal. Petter would have come here in a few days to complete the build-up to this year's Tour de Ski," said coach, Egil Skinstad, to Aftenbladet on telephone, from Seiser Alm.

He stressed that this will not affect this year's season.

"Now we will arrange a memorial down here and take a few days off to let everyone recover from the shock, before we continue the run as normal."

Skinstad has no theory about who might be behind the horrific murder.

"No. Petter was an incredibly positive and jovial person who was liked by everyone around him. I really hope that the person responsible is found as soon as possible."

Trainer and father Ole-Petter Jansrud said to Aftenbladet that the whole family is in shock, and he asks for understanding in the difficult times ahead.

"We'll gather at the farm on Inderøy and remember Petter. What we need now is time and quiet to find ourselves again and support each other."

Jansrud also said that Petter's brother, Hans, has already decided to skip this season and is on his way home, from Seiser Alm.

JANUARY 30, 2012: MORNING

Kᴜʀᴛ Hᴀᴍᴍᴇʀ ᴀᴡᴏᴋᴇ ᴏɴ ᴛʜᴇ ᴄᴏᴜᴄʜ ɪɴ Vᴏʟᴠᴇᴠᴇɪᴇɴ 11, to the sound of someone ringing the doorbell. His head felt like it was about to explode. As he opened his eyes, he discovered, to his amazement, an empty bottle of Jack Daniels on the coffee table.

A new ring sounded from the outer corridors.

What the hell was I doing last night? He got up and staggered out into the outer corridors.

When he opened the door, he rested his gaze on a curvy-figured female with shoulder-length, raven black hair, big dark eyes, and dark red lips.

"Hey." She smiled.

"Hey. Do you know what time it is?"

"Ten to eleven," she replied, flustered after looking at the silver watch on her arm.

"Shit. I should've been at work two hours ago! Do you have a car?"

She nodded, and he noticed a silver Passat in the driveway. As he put on his overcoat in the hallway, he realized that his phone was in his pocket. He picked it up and discovered five missed calls from Editor Karlsen.

"Yes, hello. Kurt here. Sorry. Overslept."

"I thought so. Had you been new, I'd have fired you on the spot. But considering yesterday's unfortunate turn of events..."

"Sorry."

Listen, I need you to figure out where the police are in this case. Talk to Dundre, the detective inspector."

"Consider it done. I'll phone you back as soon I know anything more."

He hung up and sat next to the woman, in the car. "Thank you for doing this. You can drop me off in the city center. Excuse me, but have we met before?"

She gave him a flurried gaze. "Lise! We met last night, remember?"

"Oh! Sorry. I had a bad day at work yesterday."

"You really don't remember, do you?" She smiled.

"Yes, I invited you over for a glass of wine, didn't I?"

"Correct."

"Is eight o'clock tonight good for you?"

"Hm. My shift is then, but I may change it."

"Fine. Then we have a deal." He shuddered at the thought.

The last woman he'd had at home for wine was Marte. His soul longed for her now. The smell of her golden hair. Her eyes that could see right through him as if he were glass. Her force of life that was expressed through her raw and merciless humor.

The rest of the drive proceeded in silence.

———

"Listen, I know you don't trust me after Trolla Brug—"

"Damn right I don't!"

Detective Inspector Dundre and Kurt Hammer sat at the head of a corner in the newly opened Starbucks on Kongens Gate Street. The sound system was playing Tord Gustavsen Trio's melancholy version of "Graceful Touch", and the smell of freshly brewed latte was floating in the air.

"Well, I had envisioned a trade," Hammer said. "If you tell me where you stand, I'll tell you what I've got so far."

"Okay. You first." Dundre leaned over the round wooden table and squinted.

"I checked the passenger list. I think the two cases are linked and that the killer was on the plane."

"Why?"

"Because he was murdered at the airport. Why would anyone go all the way out there to do it?"

"Well, it is conceivable that someone did it just to get you to come to that conclusion."

"But then they must've had an exceptionally strong motive."

"Well, I guess you'd be right about that."

"And I think it was a man, because it was done in the men's room."

"Well, that... why do you think the cases are linked?"

"Come on, Dundre! Two murders in Trondheim, in under a week? Fair enough that the first murder technically happened in Stjørdal, but that doesn't make it any less weird."

Dundre flashed an oily smile. "Well, I must say, that's an interesting theory you have, Hammer."

"And you? Where do you guys stand?"

Dundre rose and put on his gray trench coat. "You'll know if you show up at the press conference in Gryta kl. 18."

"Have I ever told you you're an asshole?"

Dundre smiled again. "I've always known you felt that way about me. See you tonight."

Hammer picked up his cell and called back Editor Karlsen.

"Yes, hi, it's me again. The bastard wouldn't give me a single thing. He said they'll have a press conference in Gryta kl. 18. Should I talk to Hansen?"

"Yes, do that. We're sending a camera team there as well, but we need coverage for the newspaper."

———

THE AUDIENCE RECEPTION area at the police station in Trondheim was seething with life. Frank Hansen and Kurt Hammer had met in good time and had found seats in front of journalists from NRK, TV2, Byavisa, Aftenposten, Klassekampen, and VG.

As Detective Inspector Roy Dundre sat, followed by Hanne Lundmo, the Chief of Police in Trondheim, and Arne Koppang, Chief of Police in Stjørdal, a hail of flashes went off from cameras which just as easily could've been lightning from the rainy sky outside.

"As you know," Lundmo brushed away a few blonde strands from her forehead, "Two assassinations have recently taken place in quick succession, in Trondheim and Stjørdal. We are currently working with a theory that the two cases are linked. Thus, we are now cooperating with police in Stjørdal to get the cases solved as soon as possible. Detective Inspector Roy Dundre will now say something about the murder that was discovered yesterday by two journalists who are currently present."

"Thanks, Hanne. As most of you probably know by now, a corpse was found yesterday in cross-country skier Petter Jansrud's house, in Byåsen. The body was quickly identified as that of the home owner. The two journalists who found the body are now checked out of the case. Currently, we are looking for a man between thirty and forty years old who may have been in the men's room with Mr. Blekstad when he was killed. We are still waiting for the exact time of death. Right now, we do not know where the offender is, but we are working on a theory that he might have been present at Mr. Blekstad's flight from Moscow. Moreover, we can confirm that yesterday, at half-past twelve, a bomb went off near Trondheim Torg. The bomb was mounted on the motorcycle of journalist Kurt Hammer, and went off as the bike was on its way here. One policeman was killed, and no one was injured."

Kurt Hammer squirmed in his seat and whispered to Hansen. "Those bastards stole my theories!"

Frank snorted. "This whole press conference is a disaster. So far, they have nothing."

Roy Dundre continued. "What happened remains a mystery. Out of consideration for the bereaved, we have chosen not to reveal personal details at this time. Now, I'll give the floor over to Arne Koppang, Chief of Police in Stjørdal."

"Thank you, Roy."

Koppang looked up from the papers he'd been studying and appeared to be nervous, as if he'd spent the whole conference figuring out what to say. Hammer thought he resembled a slightly younger version of union leader Arne Johannesen, with a dark beard and a police cap.

"As Roy pointed out, we are looking for a man between thirty and forty years of age, and will now have additional emergency personnel at Værnes airport to look for suspicious people or activity. Then, if Hanne has nothing more to say, I think we're open for questions?"

She nodded, and several arms were immediately hoisted into the air. Hanne Lundmo pointed to a tall man with short blond hair who looked a bit like Eminem.

"Hi." He stood. "Jo Skårderud here, from Klassekampen.

Roy, I was wondering if you could say whether you believe that the bomb and the killings are linked in some way?"

"Currently, we have no information to indicate that this is the case, no. And for the record, journalist Hammer is preliminarily checked out of the case as well."

Next, Lundmo pointed at Kurt Hammer.

"Hammer here, Aftenbladet. Can you explain why you'd organize a press conference when you don't have any relevant information to share?"

Roy Dundre turned red as a tomato, and in between all the flashing from the cameras, one could hear some people giggling.

"As a former police investigator," Roy said, in an icy tone, "you of all people should appreciate how difficult such cases can be without a single shred of evidence!"

———

"He had a Freudian slip," Hansen said, in the car on the way to Volveveien at Nardo.

"I think you may be right," said Hammer. "They'll probably find fingerprints and DNA evidence. But it doesn't mean anything unless they have someone to tie it to."

"At least we have a front-page story. I expect you'll have it written by the end of the evening?"

"I'm expecting a visit, but she won't stay for long, I think."

"Oh?"

"I got a Lise at the door this morning. Apparently, I'd invited her over for a glass of wine."

"How great! I think you may need it."

"Watch your mouth." Hammer slammed the door behind him, in the pouring rain.

JANUARY 30, 2012: NIGHT

"Sorry," were the first words out of Frank Hansen's mouth as he crossed the threshold of his apartment in Eirik Jarls Gate.

"I'm not angry with you, just very disappointed. I stopped being angry a week ago," a voice announced, from the bathroom.

Frank threw off his jacket in the outer corridors. "Yes, but dear..."

He went, with a conciliatory gait, into the combined living and kitchen room and further out into the bathroom, with black and white tiles.

Alexandra lay in the ceramic tub, with bubbles up to her chin. Her blonde hair, which had turned dark from the water in the tub, flew in all directions as she turned to stared at him.

"What was it this time?"

"Press conference. I told you before I left!"

"Did they say anything interesting?"

"To be honest, they could just as easily have saved themselves. They had nothing to offer. Kurt fortunately put Roy Dundre, the detective inspector, in his place."

"Kurt, Kurt, Kurt! I think he's the only thing I hear about these days."

Frank smiled. We've been working together a lot, recently. I hope the police find out who's behind these murders soon so that things can calm down."

"You have to watch out for him. I know the type. How do you he wasn't responsible for killing Jansrud? Cos I'm assuming it wasn't you?"

Frank sat on the stool next to the tub. "How can you say such a thing, dear?"

"You were questioned by the police! I'm going to have a child. I couldn't stomach being a single mom."

"You won't have to be, I promise you." He bent down and kissed her forehead.

———

KURT HAMMER PEERED through the liquor cabinet in the living room of Volveveien 11A. He frowned. It was almost empty, but fortunately not without a bottle of Chianti Classico. He took it out, placed it on the coffee table and went to the kitchen to throw away the empty Jack Daniels bottle from the night before.

When the doorbell rang, he'd already finished his first glass.

"Hi!" Lise had put on a little black dress, displaying her large cleavage.

In her hand she held a stack of small forget-me-nots.

"Hi! Oh, how nice, you really didn't need to bring anything."

She flashed a shy smile. "I grow them myself. Don't worry about it. Thought maybe they could cheer up the apartment a little, since you mentioned that it had felt so lonely after Marte died."

Hammer let her come in and helped her take off her black leather jacket.

"Hm, yes, I suppose I did."

He took the flowers, showed her into the living room, then put the flowers in a glass vase shaped like a Forget-Me-Not he had given Marte as an engagement present. The memories of their first date flooded back.

He'd gone into Tulla Fischer in the city center, with a bouquet of red roses he'd managed to pick up just before the florist closed.

"Oh, thank you. They're gorgeous," she said.

As he sat at the table, she whispered in his ear, "Forget-Me-Not is my favorite. Remember that."

Then she laughed her distinctive trilling laugh and looked at him tenderly with her blue almond eyes.

"Is there something wrong," Lise asked, from somewhere far away.

He turned and looked at her strangely. "No, nothing wrong. I just became so fascinated by the beautiful flowers.

"I think you needed them." She pointed at the plastic-covered window behind him."

"Oh, that... happened a long time ago. To be honest, I haven't had time to fix it."

Her dark eyes glistened in the light from the candle burning on the coffee table.

"I probably shouldn't ask, but you never told me what happened to Marte."

Kurt pulled a cigarette from the inner pocket of his canary-yellow dress shirt, brought it to his mouth, and pulled out an old Zippo lighter from his left pocket. With a slow, seemingly contrived movement, he lifted it up to the cigarette, flipped open the lid, lit the cigarette, and sucked on it for a while. Then he ambled over to the burgundy leather Chesterfield chair on the other side of the coffee table, sat and poured Chianti Classico in her wineglass, then took a gulp.

"I had been at Trolla Brug. They'd bought heroin from the Russians and I had enough evidence to put them behind bars. When I came home, the window had been shattered and she was already dead in our bed, together with our kid. Fortunately, there was enough heroin to get them sentenced for ten years each."

"Them?"

"Hell's Angels. They robbed me of everything."

She got up, walked around the table and looked into his eyes.

"Wrong. You have me." She kissed him, passionately.

Two glasses later, they lay entwined, in the bedroom. As she tore off his sweater, a shock burst through him.

"Damn, Lise, I've got a story to write!"

NO LEADS FOR POLICE

BY KURT HAMMER

At the press conference at the police headquarters in Trondheim last night, it emerged that the police are currently hunting for a man. He is between thirty and forty years of age. However, they are otherwise without any leads in this week's murder cases at Værnes Airport and in Trondheim.
The man is believed to be behind the murders of lawyer Christian Blekstad and cross-country skier Petter Jansrud. The police are still awaiting the precise time of death for the two murder victims.
It also emerged that police consider the bomb that went off inside journalist Kurt Hammer's motorcycle, near Trondheim Torg yesterday, a mystery. The incident led to a police officer being killed (see pp. 20-25), and is supposedly not linked to the two killings.
Detective superintendent Roy Dundre confirmed that the police in Trondheim and Stjørdal have begun cooperating to resolve the two cases as quickly as possible. In the weeks ahead, Værnes airport will be under surveillance by police forces in

Stjørdal, which will be on the lookout for suspicious people and activities.

ERIK LARSEN

THE FIRST MEMORY ERIK LARSEN HAD OF MOTORCYCLES was his father's Harley Davidson Night Train FXSTBI with chromed camshafts. Almost every evening after work was spent screwing on it and polishing it.

"One day it'll be yours," his father said, proudly, as he dropped Erik off at school.

Erik smiled as he climbed off and saw that many students were standing in a huddle, watching the roaring monster.

When he came home from the eighth grade that afternoon, his father didn't return from work. Usually he'd be home before Erik's mother. This day, they ate dinner alone.

"Where's Dad?"

His mother's green eyes shone with uncertainty at him.

"I called his job, but he didn't pick up. He's probably on his way home."

When Erik finished his homework on the second floor, he had yet to smell tobacco smoke from the hallway or hear the sounds of his dad's screwdriver from the garage.

He closed his books, went down the creaking stairs, through the wall-to-wall carpet clad hallway and into the living room.

"Where's Dad?"

His mother paced around the parquet floor, dressed in a light blue vernal dress.

"I don't know, honey. I've called the police."

That evening, Erik couldn't get to sleep. A little past midnight, the police phoned. His father's bike was found by the Aker River, without any clues except blood stains on the seat.

A few days later, it was front-page news. *A Man Found Dead at the Bottom of the Aker River, Presumably Killed in a Gang Shooting.* Little did he know then that his father's funeral would also turn out to be his mother's, and that men with bearded faces and tattooed arms, wearing motorcycle suits and vests, were going to attend the funeral. The doctors said she had suffered from heartache.

If Erik had been a normal teenager, and the men who gathered at the funeral had been ordinary men, child welfare would've taken care of him. But when a CPS representative met up with Erik at the small wooden house with a garden patch and a garage, in Grønland, Oslo, he found it locked and stripped of its fixtures. The only way he knew anyone had stayed there was the stinking corpse of a cat on the stairs outside. The red-sprawling coat was without blood stains. The only indication that the animal hadn't retired naturally was that its green eyes were bulged out of a bloated face.

———

HOLY SHIT. What a whore. Did she really try to kill me because I called her by her real name?

Erik Larsen was no stranger to killing. But something about the fifty-five-kilo creature with dark fluffy hair and green almond eyes prevented him from squeezing the crap out of her, as he'd done with the red-sprawling monster many years earlier. Perhaps it was because she was lovely. Or because she had tried to do it to him. She was an equal.

Instead, he knocked her unconscious and dressed her naked body in the bedcover. He got dressed, grabbed the bedspread in one hand and threw it across his shoulders as though it was a sack of potatoes. After he'd carried her through the hallway, into the elevator, and through the hotel's reception, he threw her into the sidecar of the black Ural motorcycle parked outside. He got onto the motorcycle and headed for a delegation of Hell's Angels members, in the abandoned shipyard that was Trolla Brug. Fifteen minutes later, he dumped her in a closed room and left her there while they discussed the situation.

"What shall we do with her?" Erik asked.

"I think we should get rid of her as soon as possible," someone said. "Why'd we bring her here?"

Erik was the most tender of them, and the one with the most sunken face. But on the other hand, he had the longest hair and beard, and then he pulled a Walther PPQ from his vest pocket and shot it in midair.

Silence.

"She knows something. She's bat-fuck crazy. She tried to kill me because I called her a whore. I suspect she might be behind the murders of the lawyer and Jansrud. Fetch her!"

Balder, the largest and the only one without hair on his head, stood and walked toward the exit. The wooden chair he'd sat on seemed to lift as he rose.

———

"Вы говорите по-английски?" *Do you speak English?*

The frail and battered body lying on the concrete floor, in the circle of large, bulky men had hair in its eyes and stared at the floor. The half-naked woman dressed in a tight-fitting, black crystal bra and a minimalist string was trembling, whether out of fear, coldness, or anger.

"Да, So-so," Olya said.

"I know you killed those men," said Erik.

"You know nothing." She spat at him.

In a fraction of a second, he had gone down on his knees, grasped her throat and stabbed his PPQ against her temple.

"Give me one good reason not to kill you," he whispered in her ear.

"Kurt Hammer," she gasped.

FEBRUARY 1, 2012

When the alarm clock rang in Volveveien 11A, Kurt Hammer almost fell out of bed. To his amazement, he discovered that Lisa was lying naked beside him.

"Up, now!"

"Zzz... huh? Are you writing again?"

"No, much worse. Funeral in Nidaros Cathedral."

"Funeral?"

"Long story. Let's just say that the last person who borrowed my Harley disintegrated, so I feel like I have to be there."

"Ouch. You want me to come?"

"If you can drive me, that would be nice, but only if you have nothing better to do."

She smiled. "I was almost dumped for work last night. Why should I have something better to do than spend the day with you? But I hope you have something else to put on than that yellow suit of yours."

He looked at her through squinted eyes. "Hm. I actually own a black suit, but I don't know if it'll fit me yet."

"Go put it on. Let me see."

Kurt reluctantly got out of bed and went over to the PAX wardrobe from IKEA which dominated one short wall of the bedroom. His black suit, which had only been used for Marte's funeral, hung amongst all her old dresses. Black really wasn't his color. After he'd ordered two canary yellow suits on the Internet, they had become all he ever wore.

"Oh, Kurt, you look really handsome." She heaved herself out of bed, in nothing but a thong, and kissed him.

"I prefer yellow, but..."

———

KURT HAD NEVER BEEN RELIGIOUS. Yet he found it hard not to feel reverent as he walked up the road to the giant cathedral, with its green roofs, mighty spires, Gothic windows, soapstone walls, and two angel-ornate signs above the wooden door that reminded all visitors that *This is the Lord's house, and these art Heaven's gates.*

As he was about to enter through the open door, he turned instinctively.

"Stay here," he said to Lise, without turning back around.

He continued down the road, which had been turned into a sea of mud in the rain. Then he continued on the grass, among soapstone and marble tombstones.

Far away in a corner, he stopped, took out a rose from the bouquet he'd bought at the Nardosenteret mall, and laid it on Marte's grave. Just then, he felt a hand on his shoulder.

"You miss her, don't you?"

Silence.

"Her grave looked so lonely the last time I was here." He turned in a single movement, with his eyes closed, his face pointing down. "Come now. We have a funeral to attend."

THE FIRST THREE rows of wooden benches in the cathedral were occupied by policemen who had come to honor their deceased colleague. The main ship was full, yet it was impossible to hear anything except the rain hammering against the painted windows and the monotonous voice of dean Ragnhild Jepsen.

"Per Eliassen was only employed by the Trondheim Police for fourteen months but had already become a treasured colleague to all those he came in contact with. The one he worked the most with was Hans Fiskå, who has described him as a reliable, warm and conscientious policeman, with a warm sense of humor and a satirical look at everyday life."

Kurt had sat with Lise in one of the rear rows, and he saw a tall, strong fellow of a policeman on one of the front rows, who sobbed and lamented.

Jepsen continued. "On the home front, he was expecting a child with his beloved Stine, who wants me to say that he was her heart. The day Per was so abruptly taken away, he would've come home to receive the news that Stine was pregnant. In such situations, life becomes meaningless. Some of you are probably thinking, *How can such things happen?* Then I like to think of the story about the man who had a dream. He dreamed he was walking along the beach with the lord. On the sky, scenes from his life were unfolding. For each scene, he noticed two sets of footprints in the sand—one for himself and one for the lord. When the last scene played out on the sky, he looked back at the footprints in the sand. He noticed that many times, there was only one set of footprints. He also noticed that it happened at the lowest and saddest points in his life. This upset him very much, so he turned to the lord and said, 'Lord, you said that once I decided to follow you, you would follow me all the way. But I have noticed that at the lowest and saddest days, there are only one set of footprints. I do not understand why you would leave me when I needed you the most.' The Lord replied, 'My precious child, I love you and would never leave you. On your days of pain and trials, I carried you on my shoulders.' This parable may be worth remembering not only for Stine, but for anyone who will know grief and bereavement now and in the future. It is written in Matthew chapter five, *Now when Jesus saw the crowds, he went up on a mountainside and sat. His disciples came to him, and he began to teach them. He said, Blessed are those who mourn, for they will be comforted. Blessed are the meek, for they will inherit the earth. Blessed are those who hunger and thirst for righteousness, for they will be filled. Blessed are the merciful, for they will be shown mercy. Blessed are the pure in heart, for they will see God. Blessed are the peacemakers, for they will be called children of God. Blessed are those which are persecuted because of righteousness, for theirs is the kingdom of heaven. Blessed are you when people insult you, persecute you, lie on you, and falsely say evil against you because of me. Rejoice and be glad, because great is your reward in heaven.* The sermon on the Mount was Per's favorite scripture in the Bible, and therefore it is so fitting on a day like this. Per was one of those who, particularly in the workplace, but also at home, hungered and thirsted for justice. So it feels extra unfair that he was so abruptly cut off. But he knew in his heart that he would receive his reward in heaven. In the end, we'll all meet again in the house of God, and that fact must comfort us in our grief and despair. Now Per's brother, Harald, has asked to say a few words."

Jepsen went down from the pulpit, and a thin, tall figure slowly stood from the front row. His footsteps echoed amongst the long arches in the ceiling. When he turned, Kurt saw that he had a big black mustache, thick black slick hair, and black eyes.

"Per was my brother, but he was also my friend." His voice was dark but wispy. "I haven't just lost one of my best friends, my children have lost the world's best uncle. Last Christmas, he invited us to his home even though he and Stine didn't really have the space. He wanted us to be together, and that says it all about Per. He was always the tough one of us, the one who took on a challenge without hesitation. So being a policeman fit him. But he had a soft interior. In the late night hours on Christmas Eve, he told me how they'd been forced to throw young people in jail at work. 'I wish them all well, he'd said. 'I just wish they hadn't vomited on me when I was going to get them out of the back seat.'"

The assembly erupted in reserved laughter.

"Yet he insisted on providing blankets and a hot thermoses to everyone in custody, when he was on duty. Today, we say goodbye to one of Trondheim's finest officers, and that pains me on more than just a personal level. But as Ragnhild Jepsen put it so nicely, we will all get our reward in heaven."

―――――

THE RAIN CONTINUED to splash down as the funeral procession left the Nidaros Cathedral and continued out to the cemetery. Kurt didn't envy family and colleagues who had to bury a loved one in such weather. He'd forgotten an umbrella, but fortunately had his fedora.

Lise seemed to freeze as soon as she came outside, and insisted on holding hands, which he reluctantly accepted. When the party came to the hole which was dug just meters from Marte's grave, Kurt sneaked his way forward to add a bouquet atop the coffin. The color reminded him of Marte at home in Volveveien, and right now he regretted that he hadn't bought white flowers.

That was when he saw it. An assembly of hairy bikers on Harley Davidson motorcycles drove up the Munkegaten Street. Before he became aware of what was about to unfold, bullets were flying everywhere. The sound of hammering machine guns mingled with the sound of screams emanating from people who were hit.

———

AT THE REMA 1000 store in Dronningensgate, Lars Guldbrandsen and Johnny Halvorsen had parked for lunch after a boring day at work. As Johnny sunk his teeth into a cinnamon swirl, a message blared from the radio.

"Calling all units! Calling all units! A black-suited gang of motorcyclists just gunned down lots of the people in Per's funeral procession. Last seen driving towards Prinsensgate!"

Before the message had finished, Lars hit the accelerator and the car lurched, causing the cup of coffee in the holder on the dashboard to leap to the floor.

"What the hell!" Johnny yelled.

"Just turn on the sirens, Johnny!"

"Who's attacking a funeral procession in broad daylight?"

"Some damn idiots."

The car sped toward Prinsensgate, and once they arrived at the tram stop, Lars and Johnny saw a black-clad horde headed towards Ila.

"Message received. The motorcyclists were just observed running towards Ila. In pursuit."

A few seconds afterward, Lars hammered on the brakes with such force that Johnny jerked forward. The car flew to the side and stopped less than a meter from the Gråkallen tram.

"Damn. I was stopped by the tram. Patrol 11C will continue toward IIa as soon as we can turn around!"

———

Erik had settled towards the back before Ilaparken. Everything went according to plan. At the roundabout after Ilaparken, he headed for Byåsen and was followed by a couple guys. All the others continued down Bynesveien, towards Trolla.

———

When patrol 11C arrived at Bynesveien 100, Trolla Brug, they saw nothing but a closed shop for motorcycle parts across the road and another patrol car parked in front of the old shipyard. Lars rolled his vehicle towards the other car and stared at the rain splashing down toward the windshield. Then he rolled down the window and stuck out an elbow while digging out a cigarette from his pocket.

"Asterix and Obelix, have you seen anything?" Lars asked.

A small man with a black goatee leaned out the window of the other car.

"Ha-ha, very funny, Lars. No, not yet. But we were told what had happened and thought we'd drive down here and check. We've received approval for the use of weapons, but thought we'd wait for backup. This is the Hell's Angels HQ, isn't it?"

"That's right. It seems very quiet here. Could they have brought their bikes inside?"

"I'm almost counting on it if they're inside. How many guys were there?"

"I'm not quite sure, but it looked like there might've been around twenty of them."

Both men looked at the old granite building, which had a bush of ivy growing up along one corner. The exterior didn't look like it ever had been restored after it was raised in the sixties, except that it had a new roof.

None of them liked the idea of storming into a potential ambush. But none of them would be the one that crept to the cross and summoned reinforcements.

"What say you, Anders, should we check it out?" said the little man with the goatee asked the giant of a man sitting beside him, while leaning on the steering wheel.

"Honestly, Ron, I think we should wait—"

Just then, they heard the sound of sirens, and soon they were flanked by a white Volvo, out of which a pissed-off Detective Inspector Dundre stepped out.

"What the fuck are you staring at?" he spewed.

He put forward a chubby arm and pointed at the rubble building. All the officers let out a collective sigh, took out their guns, and went out in the rain. With Roy Dundre in front, all five with weapons in hand rushed towards the gray stone building. Dundre slowly opened one of the green metal doors. Even with the sound of the rain splashing against the ground, one could hear a creak as the door was opened.

Once inside, a collective gasp was let out by the group of policemen upon realizing they had encountered twenty-one black-clad motorcyclists standing in front of their bikes, with their hands in the air and as many machine guns in a pile in front of them.

———

"KURT, Kurt, you mustn't swim out too far!"

"I know, Mom!"

The salty water beat against him as he hit the surface with his face first. The sound of gulls and cousins Anne and Kristine at his heels told him that summer had arrived.

"First out to the raft!" Kurt yelled.

"That's not fair. You started the sooner us!"

Back on the rocks in the bay, his father was sitting with a cigar in his mouth, as he always did when uncle Gunnar was present, and was clapping enthusiastically. So was Uncle Gunnar. But it was usually Kurt who was first to reach the raft. He never made a big deal out of it when victory was sealed, just crawled up on the raft, which was anchored a hundred meters out into the bay, and lay down to stare up at the blank sky. They could remain like that for hours and talk about everything and nothing. Eventually, Uncle Gunnar would light a fire back at the shore, a bonfire so big that the other families in the bay either flocked to them to grill or sought shelter for the heat.

That's when Kurt used to let them jump in the water first, usually Anne before Kristine because she was the oldest and had the longest hair, before he himself ventured out and let the now slightly warmer water cool down his even hotter body. Back at the shore, they used to grill sausages and marshmallows until the sun went down.

For some reason, those memories filled Kurt as he hit the grassy lawn of the cemetery. The sight of his fedora meters ahead of him brought him back. He strained to rise, and then checked that everything was okay. He couldn't feel any pain, just fear heightened by the sound of screaming and swearing around him.

When he finally stood, he remembered her. "Lise!"

All the other people who either were lying or standing half-upright paid him no mind. He ran with an obsession until he laid his eyes on her. She lay on the ground, her hair smeared with blood. Her voluptuous body which had woken up with him that morning, was still. Her eyes, black as coal, had been tinged with death.

He felt a pair of hands grab him as he was about to fall down on his knees.

"You're coming with us!"

———

"Would you like some whiskey?" Kurt asked.

"No, thanks. I don't drink at work."

A cute blonde wearing a long-sleeved black dress was standing in the living room of Volveveien 11A, watching Kurt Hammer with a sheepish expression.

"No? Well, I guess I'll have to drink all by my lonesome, then. Tell me again, why are you here?"

"Roy went to try and locate the bikers. He believes they were looking for you. He insisted that you not be kept alone."

Kurt Hammer sat in his Chesterfield chair behind him, lit a cigarette and let himself be embraced by the alcohol's safe grip. *How the hell could I have managed to lose her?*

"What are you thinking about?"

Kurt noticed that the blonde had settled in the chair opposite.

"She came to me. All alone. It was my responsibility to take care of her, damn it!"

He placed his glass of whiskey on the coffee table and lifted the bottle of Jack Daniels to his mouth.

FEBRUARY 2, 2012: MORNING

"Has something happened?"

"Not since we arrived, no."

A man of two meters stood on the gravel driveway outside Volveveien 11A, and peered outside the front door. He had been joined by the blonde, in a long-sleeved black Armani gown, with Swarovski crystals along her torso.

"How is he?"

"What to say? He asked if I wanted to drink, and proceeded to down a bottle of Jack Daniels when I said no. He fell asleep after most of it was empty."

The man chuckled.

"No wonder, considering what's happened. If I hadn't stood here, I'd have probably tried catching the bastards, or gone home with a bottle myself."

The blonde shook her head. "If it really was him they were looking for, it might be just as well we are here and not on a manhunt."

The two took a last peek before she went in and closed the door behind her.

———

Kurt Hammer was awakened by the vibration of his phone in his jacket pocket. As usual, his vision was blurred and his head felt like it was about to explode. He knew that the previous day must've been brutal, though the only thing he could think of was getting a hold of something to drink.

He got up, brushed away a few strands of hair from his forehead, and stumbled toward the kitchen. There, he bowed towards the tap over the sink, opened his mouth, and put the water on full blast. Then he lifted the cell phone out of his pocket. The screen on his phone shone on him. One unread text message. It was in Russian. A quick look at Google Translate showed him, *Meet me in an hour at the Trondheim hotel, room 662.*

———

The bus from the Nardo mall was overcrowded, as usual. Kurt had barely set his foot inside before he remembered why he loved riding a motorcycle. The wind in his face. The adrenaline that came when the needle went past one hundred. The joy of not having to wait for the bus. Moreover, he hated having to share space with others, even when he sat next to the first and best D-cup he could find.

Just as he'd been seated, a baby in the seat behind him began belting, while his mobile vibrated.

"Hammer!" Karlsen said. "It's eleven and you're not at work yet. What really happened yesterday?"

"Sorry, overslept again. A gang of bikers attacked us yesterday."

"Oh, my God. You were there? Just... you don't have to get

64

to work, but it'd be nice if you showed up today or tomorrow for an interview."

Kurt grinned. "Yeah. I guess I'm starting to become a local celebrity at this point, so that should be doable."

"Hope you're doing fine."

"Well... the woman I was with was shot and I was fetched home with a police escort. But everything taken into consideration, I guess I'm doing okay."

"Shit. Sorry."

"Right now, I'm mostly pissed. I hope the police will catch them and that we get to hang them out to dry."

"We will, Kurt. This is what we're working for."

"Yes, I know. But I got another incoming call here, so talk to you later."

Kurt sighed and reminded himself to have a beer when he got to the city center.

"Hammer!" said Hansen. "Kurt, hell, are you all right?"

"Under the circumstances, yes. But I'm going to keep away from work today."

"So you didn't hurt yourself?"

"She and I were shot, Frank! It was my responsibility to look after her. She died right before my eyes."

"Want to grab a beer? I'll come and meet you at once."

"Maybe tonight. I'll call you, okay?"

"Okay. Just don't sit down to drink alone?"

"I won't."

When the bus stopped in Kongens street thirteen minutes later, Kurt exited and immediately continued to Cafe Dublin, his regular pub in Trondheim.

The brown wood and brick interior of Cafe Dublin had always attracted Kurt Hammer. Moreover, they had an excellent selection of beer. So he went there to seek shelter from the rain and lessen the growing pain in his abdomen. When he'd emptied a glass of Guiness, staring out at Prinsensgate street, a message materialized in Russian, on his phone.

"I'm coming," he murmured.

———

THE TRONDHEIM HOTEL, room 662, was sparsely furnished with a double bed, a square puff, and a TV in front of the bed. In a corner, stood a chair. Behind it, a lamp.

"Why'd you invite me?" Kurt hung up his jacket.

She watched him from the bed, her brown eyes full of life. "Because I liked your company." She smiled at him with her full lips. "You're not like other men I've met," she confessed as he snuggled up to her on the bed.

He kissed her lightly on the cheek and began to massage her. "What's your name?"

"Lola Bunny."

"No, I mean your real name."

As he said it, he saw a flame of terror in her eyes, as if the words had penetrated her chest. Within a fraction of a second, she had put her hand in the bedside drawer beside the bed.

"Oh, no, you don't." He grabbed her throat.

———

ERIK DROVE down in the parking garage at Trondheim Torg. His chances of being caught were great. But on the other hand, it was possible that the police thought they had caught all of them.

As he dribbled his Harley around the underground bend, he got some suspicious glances from a passing driver, but he would soon be gone, anyway.

When he had parked in a corner, he walked up the way he

came, as calmly as he could while his heart pounded. At the bus stop on Prinsensgate Street, he went inside to seek shelter from the rain. He took a mobile phone out of his leather pants and dialed a number. His fingers trembled as he hit the last keys.

———

Kurt Hammer had been sensitive to pain for as long as he could remember. He suspected that it was much of the reason why he drank. But his drinking was so out of control that he had stopped looking for reasons.

The pain that surrounded him at the moment was still so violent that if he'd been able to think rationally, he would've thought that he was going to remember it for the rest of his life.

Olya cast a horrified glance around the room she was in. Within seconds, the window smashed, followed by the mirror in the outer corridor, into a million tiny fragments. Some landed on the floor. Others disappeared into thin air. Still others cut into the skin on the legs, abdomen, face. Like projectiles made of crystal, they paralyzed her with a pain she had never known before.

The last thing she felt before becoming unconscious was her body breaking and the dissolving floor beneath her.

TERROR IN TRONDHEIM!

BY FRANK HANSEN

Just past two o'clock yesterday afternoon, a bomb exploded near Trondheim Torg.
The Trondheim hotel and Trondheim Torg, which are wall-to-wall, were badly damaged by the explosion that blew out all the windows within a kilometer radius.
So far, twenty people are confirmed dead and about thirty have been transported to St. Olav's Hospital for treatment of extensive damage. Dagbladet's political editor, Marie Simonsen, expressed concern over the incident.
"While it isn't currently possible to speculate who is behind this or any motives, I am afraid that we could be looking at a new national crisis, in line with Utøya."
Aftenbladet's political commentator Morten Brügger agrees. "I was on my way to Trondheim Cathedral School to drive my son to a dentist appointment when it happened. Even inside the car I could hear a big bang. And when I stopped and looked out the window, I saw a black cloud of smoke. I actually don't remember what went through my mind then. Presumably, I

thought of my son. But this is definitely a tragedy not only for Trøndelag, but for the whole of Norway.

FEBRUARY 2, 2012: DAY

I know who killed them. Meet me at the Trondheim hotel. Kurt—

FRANK DIDN'T HAVE TO READ THE WHOLE MESSAGE BEFORE he jumped up and raced through Aftenbladet's newsroom and out into one of the cars. Even before he was there, he could make out smoke on the horizon.

"What the hell is going on now?"

He didn't have to wait long to find the answer. Once he arrived, the whole of Trondheim Torg and the Trondheim hotel was surrounded by fire trucks and ambulances. Detective Inspector Dundre sat with the door open in a police car parked in front of the entrance to McDonalds.

He yelled into a cell phone. "... send more reinforcements, now! Massive destruction. Unknown number of casualties..."

"What's going on?" Frank asked Dundre.

"My God, Frank, can't you see I'm busy? I don't know what's happened, but it looks like a bomb went off. Are you the first reporter on the scene?"

"I came here to meet Kurt."

"Kurt! Was he here?"

"I got a message saying that he knew who killed—"

"Oh, my God." Dundre pointed.

Inside, Kurt was among a large crowd of other people carried out to an ambulance, bruised, with bloody clothes and swollen eyes.

"Shit, Kurt!"

"Are you a relative?" Paramedics eased him into the ambulance and took in the sight of the agitated journalist with stoic calm.

"He's a colleague. A friend!"

"Do you know if he has someone else?"

"No, not really."

"No? Well, I guess you'll get to tag along to the hospital."

Frank sat in the ambulance and watched as a tall, bald man in a red coat noted that Kurt was unconscious but that his heart was functioning properly.

———

Alexandra screamed and screamed as Frank supported her down the stairs, from the apartment.

"Shit! Aaahh!"

"So then, this will be all right. The car's parked right outside."

Frank didn't like the sound of his own voice—hollow and sparse, as if he had any idea what she went through.

After what felt like an eternity, they found themselves at the end of a white, sterile room at St. Olav, where Alexandra was lying in a hospital bed made of metal, holding the handle dangling from the ceiling. The sounds that came out of her mouth weren't hers, as if an animal had taken residence in the normally relaxed creature with which he'd fallen in love.

"Push, push, push," chanted the chubby, older midwife with gray hair, as she waved her arms like she was at a football stadium.

"How soon—"

"Shh!" said the midwife. "She's just a few centimeters open yet."

"Maybe it's best if I—"

"Shut up!" Alexandra screamed.

Frank Hansen stared in disbelief at his fiancée and silently retreated.

Outside in the hallway, he ended up playing Wordfeud on his phone, moving the pieces but unable to concentrate on forming words.

What was it Kurt had said? It had to be a man, because the first murder occurred in the men's room? And it couldn't be someone from Trondheim, because who would go out to...

Thoughts raced around in his head. He sat, petrified, for a few minutes, until all the pieces finally fell into place, as if Pandora's box had suddenly closed and sucked away all the universe's devilry from whence it came.

He stood and began to move, first slowly, then faster and faster, in the direction of the hospital's information desk.

"Where's Kurt Hammer?"

"He's in the emergency room. I don't know if he can have visitors right now. Are you a relative?"

"Yes, I'm next of kin, damn it! I'm the only one he has. Furthermore, it's about evidence in a murder case that might be found on his phone."

The woman sighed. "I'll call, but it may take some time. As you can see, there's chaos here right now."

Frank sighed and sat next to a woman in her mid-thirties,

who had a little girl on her lap. The girl looked as if she could be around six years old, with long blonde hair, blue eyes, and a blue skirt. Frank couldn't help but think if this was how his child was going to look in a few years.

"Where's Dad?" the little girl asked.

"He's in the emergency room, dear. He may not be able to see us, but the doctors and the good nurses are doing their best to take care of him."

"Will he go to heaven, Mom?"

"Oh, dear." The woman began crying almost imperceptibly as she clutched the little one on her lap.

Frank's thoughts circled around his own father. He had been eight years old when he'd come home from school and found his mother crying at the kitchen table. Her face had been buried in her graceful hands.

"What's wrong," he'd whispered to her.

"Dad, he... there's been an accident on the highway," she replied.

Frank hadn't managed to utter another word. He had just run up to his room and lay in bed and cried for hours.

From that day on, he had always harbored an unhealthy respect for traffic, whether he was in a car or on foot.

"Don't worry, Mom, it'll be okay," said the girl.

"I'm not afraid, dear, just a little sorry."

"It's going to be all right," Frank said, without thinking.

Both turned and looked at him.

"I'm... waiting to visit a good friend of mine. He's unconscious, but I can't

believe that it isn't going to go well."

The little girl took his hand, looked at him and smiled.

Frank smiled back and was overcome by overwhelming fatigue.

———

"Pardon?"

"Huh? Wow, I must've dozed off."

Frank quickly corrected himself when he realized he'd fallen asleep on the shoulder of the mother with the little girl on her lap.

She smiled. "It's fine. I was almost falling asleep myself. I was just saying that the lady from the information desk came and said that your friend is in emergency room 336. He's stable but unconscious."

"Oh, thank you! And what about you. Have you heard anything?"

Silence.

"He's being operated on. One lung collapsed, and he's badly bruised. I think he broke his leg, too. The doctors are doing what they can."

Frank gave her a hug.

"Look, here's my number." He pulled out a business card from his jacket pocket. "Call me if there's anything I can do for you. Anything."

"Thank you!"

Inside room 336, Kurt Hammer was connected to a heart monitor, with one leg held up in a shin guard. His hair was crudely cut, which made way for a large scar on the upper part of the forehead. Frank counted twenty stitches. He sat next to the hospital bed.

"Damn, Kurt. We need you back at work. I need you. She's here, isn't she? You smart bastard. I never would've found her without you."

He looked around. Kurt's canary yellow suit jacket was hanging on a coat stand in a corner. Frank stood and fished Kurt's cellphone out of the jacket pocket.

"I'm borrowing this. I—"

The heart monitor started beeping.

Frank ran to the door. "Hello? Anyone? He's flatlining, damn it!"

A nurse came running, followed by a physician.

"What did you do?" asked the physician.

"I didn't do anything. Just told him he had to come back."

The doctor tore up the white shirt and revealed Kurt's hairy chest before he hid it again with two black pads.

"Ready!"

Kurt's body jumped as the defibrillator sent power into it.

"One, two, three, four, five."

One of the nurses came over to Frank and pulled him toward the door.

"Will he—"

"Come now, you can't be here."

As Frank went out in the hallway, it struck him. *Alexandra!* He sprinted through the corridors, from the emergency room to the delivery room. Outside the delivery room, he was greeted by the elderly midwife.

"Congratulations, it's a girl!"

He smiled. "Thank you!"

She stepped aside and let him open the door, and he poked his head in.

"Get out! I don't want to see you."

Frank Hansen withdrew silently and shot a furtive glance at his daughter, who was red, nude, with a head covered in black hair as she sucked on her mother's breast.

———

SOMEONE HAD BEEN THERE. For how long, he didn't know. Or how long ago it was. But someone had been there recently, was his opinion, and they'd been calling him to service. It felt like his body was penetrated by millions of needles as something came back to life deep inside him.

First, his heart began to beat. Gradually pumping blood through the veins and up to the brain. He opened his eyes wide.

"Olya? Hello? Anyone? Where's Olya?"

FEBRUARY 3, 2012

"Who are you?"

Nurse Viktoria looked up with her honest blue eyes, at two uniformed muscle men who looked like they'd come straight from the nearest fitness center. She tried to seem skeptical, empowering, but was afraid they would look right through her.

"Wait here. I'll *attempt* to talk to the chief physician."

How typical of the police, coming here in the middle of the worst crisis since July 22, demanding to talk to patients hovering between life and death.

Chief Physician, Polskaya, straightened his glasses. He had just eaten a bowl of soup after completing an eighteen-hour surgery, and was about to go home to sleep, when Anna knocked on his office door.

"Hey, nice to see you again." She smiled, shyly.

"Thank you." He smiled back at the young, busty nurse with blonde curls.

They both had needed a break from work the last time they met in the break room.

"There's a couple cops here. They're asking to interview the patient in room 43. They say she's named Olya Volkova."

Polskaya snorted. "What the hell are they thinking? Coming here at ten o'clock in the morning to interview a terminally ill patient. When I moved from Russia, it was—"

"Because you wanted to escape the madness. I know. Shall I do it, or will you talk to them yourself?"

"I'm on my way home anyway, so I can do it on my way out." He enjoyed being able to show steadfastness in her presence.

When he came out, the two men were seated on a bench, apparently unaffected by what was happening around them. A television in a corner showed NRK, which had broadcast a live newscast throughout the past day, exclusively centered around the events surrounding Trondheim Torg.

A clearly affected Jon Gelius, in his abraded Arendal Dialect, concluded that, *"Police are currently looking for a man in his thirties, with black clothes and medium-length hair. He is suspected of being behind the bombing as well as having a connection to the shooting drama the day before. Any motive is still unclear, but police have issued a press release stating that the man is considered armed and extremely dangerous. Therefore, they ask that everyone exercise great caution and immediately call the police upon suspicion. Everywhere, doctors and nurses are stressed, often crying, relatives are racing in all directions."*

The two uniformed men arose only when Polskaya had come right up to them.

"Chief physician..."

"Polskaya."

"Pleasure. I'm detective Martin Skaar, and this is my colleague Brede Wiberg. We are here to interview your patient Olya Volkova. She is a suspect in a case."

"Unfortunately, that's impossible. She's still in danger after being exposed to serious cranial trauma, and is now hovering in and out of consciousness."

"Can you give us a call as soon as she is conscious again?" said Skaar.

Polskaya swallowed a snarl. "No. But if you come back in a week, I can tell you whether she's stable enough that I think it's justifiable that she can be interviewed."

The detective cast an annoyed glance around the room, as if to see if he could spot other obvious idiots.

"Well, maybe we'll come in about a week, maybe before. It would be a shame if we had to come back with a court ruling..."

"That doesn't matter, as long as she is in my custody." Polskaya shook the reluctant police officer's hand. "Now I'm going home to sleep. Good day."

———

OLYA OPENED HER EYES. Her body was drenched in sweat and shaking. Something terrible had happened, though she couldn't...

She shrieked. Her lungs screamed out in pain as she'd filled them with air, but they still had to be functional, because the sound that came out surprised even her. It was filled her with memories of the room that had collapsed around her.

A nurse burst through the door. "Is everything okay? It's good that you have awakened."

The slim, blonde creature came up to Olya, sat beside her and took her hand. Olya spoke to her in English, with a sluggish Russian accent.

"Kurt Hammer. Я хочу. Is he here? I must talk to him."

"He's here, but sleeping. And I don't think you're in any state to—"

"*Чёрт*. Shit."

She grabbed the nurse's shoulder and got up out of bed. The nurse tried to hold her back but had to settle for supporting her as she set foot on the floor.

"Are you okay?"

"Where Kurt Hammer?"

The nurse sighed and gripped around her arm. When they entered the hallway, many eyes widened at the sight of a thin girl with curls, side-cut with fifteen stitches along the side of her head, who looked like a Spaniard but swore in Russian and seemed as if she could fall over at any moment.

"I'm sorry," the nurse said to Chief Physician Polskaya, when he passed them in the hallway. "She insisted."

He smiled and turned to Olya.

"*Все нормально?*" Is everything okay?

"*Да. Где* Kurt Hammer?" Yes. Where is Kurt Hammer?

He stared at her in amazement, as if he couldn't fathom what the drunken journalist could have done to get this young lady to exhibit such energy and willpower, but ultimately considered the situation to be harmless and pointed towards a door surrounded by two policemen.

"*Он там*. He's there."

"*Спасибо,*" she muttered as thanks, and dragged the poor nurse along with her.

———

A KNOCK CAME from the other side of Editor Karlsen's door.

"Yes? Come in."

"Hi." Frank Hansen looked like a wreck.

He had big bags under his eyes after a week of too-little sleep, and Karlsen suspected that he'd gained five to ten kilograms.

"Is it okay if I take time off for the rest of the day to go to Stjørdal if I promise to look for the bomber?"

"She wants to be with her mother, huh? That's what having a family's like."

"Just me. She's already gone."

"I see?"

"That's what I suspect. She's not answering my calls after I wasn't there during the birth because I was looking for Kurt's cell phone."

Karlsen lifted his eyes from the screen and blew a huge smoke ring into the room.

"Speaking of which, you can go if you stop by the hospital to find out how Kurt is doing. It can't hurt to see if he has a story either, huh? Cursed, too, that you were able to figure out who was behind the killings without having a story to go along with it."

"Well, we've got no story yet, but everything is pointing towards her."

"Kurt knows. I can feel it. The story of the century is waiting for us. And don't worry. If Alex leaves you, she's dumber than I thought."

"Uh, sure, boss. I'll leave, then."

Karlsen's gaze had already drifted back to the screen. He waved his cigar to indicate that he was finished with the conversation.

———

OUTSIDE ROOM 336 at St. Olav's ICU, Frank Hansen was forced by two police officers to show his ID before he got to go inside. Inside the room, Olya was sitting on a chair next to Kurt's bed. The room was naked except for a vase of lilies from Aftenbladet which were on the table beside the chair.

Frank stared at Olya as he entered the room, as if she was a mix between a ghost and a monster.

"It isn't what you think," Kurt said, when he noticed Frank's gaze. "Can you wait outside?"

Frank closed the door without saying a word. After two hours, a blond nurse went through the door before coming out again with Olya. Frank avoided eye contact but couldn't free himself from wondering how a slender, young woman could've been able to have done what he assumed she had done.

"She confessed, Kurt stated, in a satisfied tone as Frank came back into the room. "She tried kill me, too, because she felt threatened. She's been through—you won't even believe it when you read the article."

"Ah, so you have a story? Karlsen was wondering how you were."

"Absolutely."

Frank sat. "I don't know what you have in mind, but you're not going to sway the man in the street's opinion of her when what she's done gets out."

"You have a lot to learn."

Frank gave him a suspicious look." "She's a triple murderer—"

"That's been pushed to her limits," Kurt whispered." Can you do me a favor?"

"Anything."

"Bring me a tablet to write on."

"No problem. I'm on my way to Stjørdal. I can call Felicia on the way."

"Stjørdal? Problems in the relationship?"

"It'll be all right," Frank said, even though he didn't believe in the voice that said it. "Good to see you're in good spirits." He stood and left.

———

CURSED, *too*, Detective Inspector Dundre thought, in his office overlooking Trondheim Central Station. Outside, the rain was hammering on the window panes and taxis were shuttling passengers to and from the station. This time, he'd just have to go himself. The two officers he sent last time were obviously not capable of anything.

He scratched his walrus mustache. *Maybe I should call Kurt.* But he soon put that idea to rest. If Olya had woken up and confided in him, she'd fall under journalistic confidentiality. Certainly, Frank Hansen had called from the hospital, given her full name, and most likely said that she was admitted. But that was also as far as cooperation went, where journalists were concerned.

Without further ado, Dundre left his office for his car, and ten minutes later he parked at St. Olav's Hospital.

———

OLYA WAS AWAKENED by a knock on her door. The room was empty. She didn't even have flowers on her bedside table.

She waved Polskaya into the room.

"How are you? I've heard your English is quite good, so I'm going to use it. Outside, is a policeman and he wants to talk to you. To be honest, you've been through a surprising recovery since you woke up three days ago, so there's a limit to how long I can keep him away on the basis of your mental state."

What was it that Kurt had said? There's no going back from this! "Let him in."

"Okay. Do you want me to stay?"

"No. I'll call you if I can't handle him."

Polskaya stood. "Okay. I'll let him in."

When he returned to Detective Inspector Dundre, Polskaya glared at him and said, "She's ready to see you, but still physically and mentally tired. She isn't fit to be detained."

Dundre nodded. "Thank you, I understand. I'm guessing she speaks English?"

The chief physician stared at him for a while. "Only if you ask the right questions."

Inside room 43, Olya immediately formed an opinion about the man who had entered. His stubble beard signified an over-worked man who still took the time to work. His eyes were small and dark, much like a badger's, and told her that this man was accustomed to tricking answers out of people, even when they didn't want to respond. Moreover, he had a huge mustache, which she suspected could be there to fool unwitting people into believing that he was a shy person who hid behind a masculine exterior.

"Can I sit?" he asked her, in poor English.

"Пожалуйста." She waved her arm toward the chair. "Please."

"You're probably aware that this is not a formal interroga-tion, so I'm going to skip the formalities. My name is Roy Dundre, and I work for the Norwegian Police. The past week has, quite frankly, been a professional nightmare for me. Two dead, in different venues, professionally done, with almost no physical evidence. The only thing that seems to connect them is that they both had a fascination for whores. And three days ago, I get a phone call where I'm told that you know who's behind it. You know what is the next thing I want to ask about?"

Olya looked down at her lap, then straight into his eyes, hers sparkling with hatred.

"They were assholes, Inspector. Violent assholes who called me a whore, a skank, and hit me." She lifted her forearm and revealed a large bruise in the shape of a crescent moon. "They got what they deserved."

"Do you mind if I take a picture?"

She said nothing, just raised her forearm again. He pulled out an phone from the pocket of his gray coat and took a picture. Then he put the phone back and took out a Ziplock bag from the same pocket, which contained a Q-tip.

"Do you mind?" He opened the bag and gave her the swab.

He noticed that her nails were painted red, white, and blue —Russia's colors. *Maybe she misses home? She must've borrowed nail polish from someone here.*

She put the Q-tip into her mouth with a smooth movement and then gave it to him.

"Thank you. You'll hear from me." He stood. "I'll speak to your doctor and make sure he tells me when you're ready to be questioned. If you leave, I'll find you."

"Where would I go." She pointed at her feet.

In the corridor, Dundre encountered nurse Viktoria. "Hey, can you tell me where Polskaya is?"

"He's in with another patient now, but I can take a message?"

"Do you know how long it'll take Olya Volkova to be able to walk again?"

"If I knew, I couldn't tell you. But nobody knows. It's possible that she's got permanent damage to her central nervous system. Unfortunately, we haven't had time to scan her yet."

"Well, have him call me as soon as he thinks she is well enough to be detained in custody. And if there's any suspicion that she's healthy enough to be able to escape..."

"Will do," nurse Viktoria said, as an alarm went off in a room. She hurried off toward it."

"He has my number," Dundre called to her.

———

"She's here, yes?"

Frank Hansen ended up standing for what seemed like an eternity looking at his mother-in-law through a half-open front door, without the two exchanging a single word.

Her shoulder-length gray hair was tied up in a knot behind her head, and her pointed made her look like she was constantly suspicious. Her faded blue eyes looked at him in a way that told him she was wondering whether or not he was an idiot or just mischievous.

"I'll check if she wants to see you," she finally said, and closed the door behind her.

After a while, she came out again, still with the same look on her face.

"Get in here. But you better act nice!"

Frank's annoyance rose with every word, and he cursed Alexandra inside for putting him through this. At the same time, maybe he deserved it? Maybe he should be looking for a new career? No, damn it! She had to realize that he loved her as well as the job.

He went into a small outer corridor and hung up his coat on one of the pegs along the wall, over which the wall was adorned by a framed aerial photo of Stjørdal. Next to the outer corridor was a small living room with a burgundy leather sofa along a wall, behind a small, round dining table. The living room was illuminated by the sun beaming through two rectangular windows overlooking a small garden plot. Between them stood a small brown dresser on top of which was lace and pictures of a young Alexandra as young as well as her late father.

Currently, Alex was sitting on the couch, nursing. Frank sat and met her eyes. An eternity passed. An eternity without words. An immersive silence which thronged around the room and pierced them.

"Can I hold her?"

Alexandra's pierced him with her glare. "All right. I believe she's satisfied now."

She lifted her daughter and approached him. He accepted her as only a new father could do, with strength and yet with ease as if he were holding a feather.

"You look terrified," said Alexandra.

"Is there something wrong with that?"

"No. It would've been a lot worse if you didn't care."

FEBRUARY 10, 2012

Roy Dundre barely had time to sit down with his morning coffee before the phone rang.

"Dundre, Trondheim Police. What can I help you with?"

"Hey, it's from forensics."

Dundre was silent.

"You know, the sample you submitted a week ago came out positive, but only for one of the deceased—Jansrud."

"Thank you. I expect you'll send the results by mail, too?"

"Of course, but it'll probably take a week's time."

"No problem. Thanks again." Dundre hung up, with a satisfied grin.

———

In another part of town, Olya Volkova had woken up less than two hours ago.

"Can you feel this?" the physical therapist asked.

"Just barely," Olya said.

Olya lay on a mat on the floor of an empty office and tried

to concentrate on what she could feel, when the smiling therapist with red curls bowed Olya's feet and struck her knees.

"Well," she was still smiling, "if you have neurological damage, it isn't substantial. But it's difficult to say for sure without scanning you."

Olya pushed herself up to stand up, using her arms. The therapist's perpetual smile and beaming optimism irritated Olya to no end.

"Will I be able to walk again?"

"It's still too early to say. But if you want, Polnaya said we can scan you today after this appointment."

Olya nodded. "Of course I want it."

"Regardless of the results, it'll take will of steel—"

Olya snorted. *Who is this lady? She's able to smile and pretend everything is okay, yet she questions my willpower. If she only knew what it took to get there, to stay alive after my mother died, she wouldn't question me.*

"You don't know me!"

"You got that right. I'm just telling you the truth."

"If power of will is what's required, I will walk again."

"Well, then lie down and stretch your legs for me. Five times each."

———

CHIEF PHYSICIAN POLSKAYA sat next to Kurt Hammer's bed, with a sheepish expression on his face.

"You don't have anyone else you can ask to go buy you alcohol?"

"When you mention it, Felicia was supposed to come from work with an iPad. I can ask her."

"If you have trouble sleeping, can I prescribe you some Valium?"

Kurt snorted. "No, thank you. I'd much rather have the bottle. Maybe writing will make it easier for me to sleep."

"Kurt."

Hammer stared at the chief physician. He wore dark brown Ray Ban glasses, possibly an attempt to conceal his moods. But on the other hand, maybe not, because his hair was tousled and the shirt he wore under his doctor's coat was stained. He reminded Kurt of an overworked father of three.

"The X-rays we took a few days ago to determine whether you've broken something... you're drinking yourself to death. Your liver is beginning to shrivel."

There was a knock at the door.

"Come in," said Kurt.

Felicia entered. Her long dark hair was soaking wet, and if she hadn't been wearing a coat, she would've probably been wet to the bone.

"Kurt!" She ran over and kissed him on the cheek. "How are you?"

"Thank you. I've had worse days. Me and Polskaya here were talking, but he was just about to leave, wasn't he?"

Polskaya nodded. "That's right." He got up and to leave, but before entering the hallway, he turned to Kurt. "Think about what I said."

"What was that about?" asked Felicia.

"Nothing. Just some doctor-to-patient stuff."

Felicia stared at him but decided not to pursue the topic further.

"Do you have a tablet for me?" Kurt said.

"Oh, that's right." She lit up as if she'd forgotten why she came.

With an elegant movement, she lifted her folding black leather Falabella bag up onto her lap and pulled out a silver iPad.

"Thanks."

"Karlsen was wondering if you had a story."

"Tell him to clear the front page." Kurt smiled.

"Oh, that's great, Kurt. I think you need to write to feel better."

"You know me too well. Can you hitch a ride to the drug store for me? I can't get to sleep."

"Ah, that's what you were talking about?"

"He would have given me Valium, but I said I'd rather take the bottle."

Felicia sighed. "All right, I'll bring something to you tonight. But now I'm going to leave so you can write."

She kissed him on the cheek, threw her bag over her shoulder, then got up and walked out.

———

"Do you need help?"

The young Pakistani MRI-nurse watched with a frightened stare as Olya crawled from the wheelchair and into the MRI scanner. Olya shook her head as the nurse approached with a hand. She finally got onto the table, on her stomach, and rolled over onto her back.

The nurse said, "You must lie very still while the machine works."

Olya just scowled, as if to say, *Does it look like I'll be able to move?*

As she was slowly led into the cylindrical opening of the large white machine, thoughts raged through her mind. *Will I be able to walk again? Will I be sent back to Russia? How long before I'm arrested?* She closed her eyes and listened to the ticking of the machine.

———

ERIK LARSEN WAS TREMBLING. He couldn't remember the last time he had done so. The fear of being discovered was still real.

As he reached the baggage transport at the security check, he was stopped by a large man in a uniform. Erik considered giving him a quick jab to his nose and leaving the scene, but behind him was a queue of at least twenty people, and in front of him were five security guards. The line consisted mostly of young families and the occasional businessman. Although they wouldn't be able to stop him, he realized that several chubby fathers in Hawaiian shirts and yuppie guys in Armani suits would be enough to hold him until the security guards could get to him.

The guard looked him up and down. "You look suspicious. Sorry, I can't let you pass. You must follow me first."

Erik said nothing but picked up his briefcase and followed the guard out of the queue.

"Name and final destination?"

"Erik Larsen. Bermuda!"

"What are you going to Bermuda for?"

"Personal travel. I'm going to visit my daughter, who I've never met."

"Are you aware that a man who fit your description was observed outside Trondheim Torg just minutes before it exploded?"

"Really? Ugh, that's so terrible. I hope you catch him soon."

"Are you or have you ever been involved with Hell's Angels?"

"Pardon? What's that? Sounds like a congregation of Satanists."

The guard sighed, clearly annoyed. "I can't let you travel if you don't answer my question. Do you want me to call the police?"

"No. For God's sake..."

Within a few seconds, Erik got up, slid his right arm slide backward and punched the guard just below the left eye. The guard jolted back and hit the wall. Before he could collect himself, Erik walked over to him and kicked him in the forehead with his military boot. The wall behind the guard's head was stained red.

———

OLYA LAY on the MRI machine and was wary of Chief Physician Polskaya, who approached with a too-positive expression.

"Hey, you. How are you?" he asked.

"Good. At least, not worse."

"I don't know... there's no easy way to say this."

"Then just say it."

"You've suffered extensive damage to your central nervous system. You need surgery, and even then I can't guarantee that you'll ever be able to walk again."

"When?"

"I don't know. If you're willing to accept that this is surgery that has a high risk of complications, I will check."

"Doctor, I'm not afraid."

Polskaya couldn't help but smile. "I can tell you one thing. With that attitude, you'll go far."

He rolled the wheelchair over to the MRI machine, then moved back to the door and looked at her as she got down off the machine, feet first, as if it were the easiest thing in the world.

FEBRUARY 12, 2012: MORNING

OFFICER LARS GULBRANDSEN SAT IN HIS CAR ON THE WAY out to Værnes. There'd been many officers there lately, which wasn't strange. But what was strange was that after one week they still had no suspects in the bombing of Trondheim Torg case.

Gulbrandsen felt that it had to be a suicide job. It was the only logical explanation. Probably an Arab. They would've been thrown out of the country, on their heads if he could decide.

Gulbrandsen was so adamant about his theory that he had shouted his thoughts to the manager, who had asked him to calm down. And after a week, they had yet to find anything that resembled Arabs or remains of any suicide bombing. Embarrassing! He was convinced that they hadn't searched in the right places.

He was awakened from his gloomy thoughts by the radio.

"Calling all units. Dangerous man on Harley Davidson heading towards Trondheim from Værnes! Killed a security guard. License number DN96650!"

"Fuck! Not again." Lars hit the accelerator and put on his sirens. "Unit 1460A on the matter. Over."

Just then, he noticed a Harley with a police car following, speeding along E6 in the opposite direction. He hammered his foot on the brake and made a U-turn, barely avoiding collision with the airport bus in the opposite lane. The bus came to a screeching stop and tipped across E6.

That's going to be a hefty municipal expense. Lars continued chasing the police car.

———

ERIK WAS FREEZING. The rain poured down on all sides, and the wind threw his hair in all directions. He had no idea where he was going, but he had to shake off the police.

———

IN ANOTHER PART OF TOWN, Under Dusken, Norway's oldest student newspaper, was vacated except for two people. This, despite being noon on a Thursday. The remaining people were receptionist Sunniva Elise Heim and culture editor Mathias Kristiansen, who was checking his mail and becoming annoyed.

"Damn, where are the culture tips when I need them." He took a gulp of coffee from the silver Statoil cup in front of him.

He was concerned that the Culture section in the next issue was going to be too small.

"Are you all right," Sunniva asked, from the other side of the cluttered room.

It was brimming with old issues of Under Dusken, PCs, dust, half-eaten ready-made boxes of food, and mugs with old coffee randomly placed on the tables.

"Yeah. But if you have tips for culture stories, they're more than welcomed."

"Sorry, I don't." Sunniva stroked her blonde curls and continued proofreading Finn Brynestad's and Emil Flakk's editorial about the useless finance board of the student union.

There was a crash sounded outside, and both of them felt a tremor in the otherwise quiet room.

Sunniva looked up at Mathias with her blue eyes. "What was that?"

"No idea, but I think we should check it out." Mathias was already on his way over to the cabinet by the wall to find a working camera.

"Agreed." Sunniva rose from her chair.

As they came out onto Singsakerbakken Street, they could hear sirens and they saw a motorcyle with wine-red paint that had crashed into Lucas, the restaurant next to the newsroom, with tire tracks leading into the building.

"Look," Sunniva screamed, and pointed to the other side of the street.

A man in a black Satyricon shirt, combat boots, and black leather pants sprinted towards the round, red building that was Studentersamfundet. He was bleeding from his left thigh and right elbow.

It must be him they're looking for. Sunniva and Mathias ran after him.

As Mathias tackled the man, Sunniva realized that he had a knife in his hand.

"Watch out!" she screamed.

Their scuffle felt like it lasted an eternity. Blood flew everywhere, and when Sunniva saw that the man was about to stab Mathias in the back, she kicked his arm. The knife flew and landed a few meters beyond the three people.

"We'll take over from here, three policemen screamed as

they came running from two police cars in the middle of the intersection in front of Lucas restaurant.

"Are you okay," Sunniva asked Mathias, as the policemen handcuffed the man and pulled him along.

Mathias had blood on his face, which looked like war paint that matched his ginger crew cut. He didn't answer, but stood and hurried to take the SLR camera from the bag he'd thrown over his shoulder. As the black-clad man was shoved into one of the police cars, Mathias took a series of photos before running to the police.

"What is this man accused of?"

"He's killed a man at Værnes, and we have reason to believe—"

"What?"

"Forget it. No comment. Are you all right, by the way? Do you wish to press charges for aggravated assault?"

"No. I tackled him, after all. But I'd very much like to know his name."

The policeman turned and had a hushed discussion with the colleague who'd been in the driver's seat of the Mercedes.

"His name is Erik Larsen," he said, finally. "We suspect he's the leader of Hell's Angels Oslo. We can't say more than that right now."

"Okay, thanks." Mathias turned and walked towards Sunniva. "I think we have a cover story for the next issue." He flashed a big grin.

———

Frank Hansen opened his eyes and looked at his ringing phone. The display showed that the time was 10:45 p.m. He considered ignoring the call, but couldn't help but feel a twinge of pity for Kurt.

"I hope you have a good reason for calling so late, Kurt."

"Yes, work. I'm writing, but I need to get something confirmed from a source. She didn't want talk on the phone."

"I've taken leave for a week. I need to be left alone with Alex and the kid."

"It won't take long, see. I just need to confirm a suspicion."

"A suspect?"

"That Christian Blekstad was a swine!"

"Okay, you got my attention. When and where?"

"Gardermoens, gate 12. She said you could come anytime. I think she's unemployed."

"Okay. I'll discuss it with Alex tomorrow. She's not going to be happy, so I can't promise that I'll be able to stay long."

"Just bring a recorder."

"Will do. How are you?"

"All right. Felicia visited and brought an iPad. I've been writing and doing research for a few hours now. She stopped by to give me a bottle a couple hours ago, so I figured I'd down it now and try to sleep."

"Sounds like an idea. Just don't drink yourself to death."

Frank hung up and lay listening to the rain hammering on the roof. From just a few hundred meters away came the distinctive sound of rotor blades cutting through the air as an ambulance helicopter landed on the roof of St. Olav. Someone had had a rough night.

Beside him lay Alexandra, who fortunately hadn't woken up. How could he have let the job come between them? Her perfect mouth, which reminded him of a crescent moon, was formed in a smile, and he shuddered at the thought of leaving her tomorrow. But he needed to keep Kurt out of it.

———

"No! You promised that you wouldn't say yes to more jobs this week."

Alexandra had gotten up and served breakfast in bed, consisting of coffee, scones, jam, and grapes on a silver platter she'd inherited from her grandmother.

Frank's chest ached, and he felt like a disobedient dog that had been playing on the couch while the owner was away.

"Sorry, dear, but it came up late last night."

"And you couldn't say no?"

He sighed. "Honestly, not really. We have bills that must be paid, and Stine must have toys, clothes. My God, we haven't even gotten a stroller."

Alexandra put the tray down on the bed and turned around.

"Where are you going?"

"To the shower. I don't want to see you before you come back, and if it takes more than a couple hours..."

"Get a job!" he shouted, and got a slamming bathroom door in return.

He immediately regretted it. Alexandra was a graduate nursing assistant, and since it was virtually impossible to get fixed position, they'd agreed that he would work and she would be home with Stine. He knew he'd gone too far. But she had to understand that it wasn't possible to live on scraps?

Frank devoured his half of the breakfast in silence, despite a nagging feeling that he didn't really deserve it. Twenty minutes later he slid his car into the parking lot in front of the whitewashed apartment complexes on Gardermoens Street. From his car, he could see that all the buildings were made of brick, and he couldn't decide whether the facades were designed in the fifties or sixties. Either way, they weren't new.

On one short side of what looked to be the oldest building, he noticed that *Trondheim Apartments* was written in large letters across a blue door. The parking lot was built around small garden patches with trees and flowers of all sizes. Had it not been for the pouring, the place would've looked real cozy.

Frank hurried out into the rain and into the oldest complex. He knocked on a door marked *A. Knutsen*. What awaited him was a woman in her mid-forties, with flabby facial features, a wafer shaped figure, and hair colored in shades of red, brown, and gray and was tight in a knot at the back of the head.

"Hey. Frank Hansen."

"Anne Berit," she said, meekly and shook his hand. Then she stepped to the side and let him enter. "Ugh, what weather. You're soaking wet. Come in and warm yourself on a cup of coffee."

"Thanks for offering."

He followed her into a small living room whose most prominent piece of furniture was a black leather sofa that looked like it'd been bought at a thrift shop.

"I assume you've been in contact with Kurt," he said.

She indicated that he should sit down while she went into the kitchen and fetched coffee.

"That's right."

Once she came out, she poured him coffee in a huge mug, from a pot she said she'd inherited from her grandmother.

"Thanks. Can you start by telling me how you knew Christian Blekstad?"

Silence. Anne Berit stared at the wooden table in front of the couch. For a moment, Frank thought that he would be forced to find a new approach.

"He was an asshole."

"Hm, yes, Kurt has expressed that sentiment, too."

"I'm a trained secretary. That is, right now I'm disabled because of him. He..." Her large blue eyes were suddenly bare.

"Take your time."

"Raped me in his office. Choked me to the point where I believed was going to die. The bastard penetrated me anally, so that I got lifelong damage. When I took it up with management, it was shushed down, as though it was a trifle. I ended up getting fired when I could no longer make it to work."

Frank opened his eyes. "Why didn't you contact the police?"

"The police don't care. Why should I have?"

Frank let silence descend upon the room, accompanied by the rain that lashed against the windowpanes in the small apartment. He took a big gulp of coffee before he continued.

"Do you think there might've been others?"

"Wouldn't surprise me," she said, flatly.

"I know this is hard, but are you willing to come forward?"

"No. I told Kurt that I'd only be interviewed if I got full anonymity."

"Hm." Frank took out a Moleskine notebook and began to write. "Then at least we have one source."

"Yes. I hope it's helped Kurt's story. He talked about what he was writing, and it didn't surprise me at all that she killed him. He deserved it."

She buried her head in her skirt. Frank couldn't decide if she was crying, but he felt deep compassion for her.

"I understand, I understand," he whispered.

On his way to Gildheim medical center to talk to Anne Berit's doctor, Frank thought about what she had said. He didn't consider himself a religious man, although he was raised in by Christian parents. *I can understand what Olya did.* But he still had trouble defending her actions. Either way, what Christian Blekstad's had done deserved to be put under the spotlight.

Frank passed the huge brown and grey concrete buildings that made up Nidar candy factory, looking for Falkenborgveien 35C. The place was hard to find, and just as he was about to give up, after passing the concrete block which constituted the main office of the ICA group five times, he took off at a big sign marked *Thoning Owesens, gate 35*. After passing a large white tin building marked *Hurtigruta Carglass*, another car place, this one with transparent roofs marked *Jensenbil.no*, and finally *Falkenborg bil A/S*, he eventually came upon a four-story colossus covered with white sheets and marked *Falkenborgen-veien 35C*.

In a note attached to one of the blue glass doors of the main entrance, he could see *Gildheim Medical Center*. Frank didn't understand how anyone could have a medical center in a place that was virtually impossible to find, but realized that he had more important things on his agenda than answering such questions.

Inside a small waiting room, he was greeted by a tall, slender creature with rich blond hair in a braid. She introduced herself as Martine Skog.

"Thank you for agreeing to meet me at such short notice," Frank said, and joined her into the office.

"Well, I got the impression of urgency, and we only have few patients today."

"Hm, that's right. The waiting room was almost empty."

"One would think that many were cold and sick in this weather, but that isn't reflected in our patients." She smiled.

"Speaking of your patients." Frank removed a piece of paper from the inside pocket of his jacket and handed it to her. "I have a statement from Anne Berit Knutsen, who claims that she sustained lifelong damage at her last place of work. Can you confirm that?"

Martine scrutinized the note carefully before she said, "Absolutely bloody terrible incident." She shook her head and sighed. "I asked her to go to the police, but she thought there was no point to it. In a way, I can understand her. I've had similar cases, yes. I can of course not discuss them with you. But as I understand it, they've all been dismissed."

Frank shook his head. "That's why it's important that this matter is receiving attention. Can you explain, in laymen's terms, what kind of damage Anne Berit sustained?"

"Well, first, major damage to the internal sphincter, i.e. the anal sphincter. Second, nerve damage resulting in bleeding and severe pain when defecating. Last, warts."

"Warts?"

"Yes. They can occur within the channel as a result of bacterial infection. It's possible that she has cancer. We're still waiting for the test results."

"My God. I can quote you on these things?"

"Of course. I only hope that your story may help prevent future incidents."

"I hope so, too." He pulled out his black Moleskine notebook and began writing.

On his way home, Frank stopped at a gas station to buy a roller burger and shrimp salad. He couldn't help but feel burning hatred at the sight of all the porn magazines, which he hadn't previously noticed.

CHIEF PHYSICIAN POLSKAYA threw his disposable gloves in the bin by the door as he left the operating room at St. Olav's Hospital. The time, he had just managed to topple five, and after an eight-hour surgery he had determined that Olya should be able to walk. Theoretically. Damage to the nervous system was unpredictable. He knew better than anyone, after over ten years of surgeries.

One of his patients had become a vegetable when she awoke. The family, of course, tried to summon him for Patient

Ombudsman, but they found that no errors had been committed. The patient had been informed about the risks, and Polskaya had taken all the necessary precautions. Nevertheless, he still had nightmares about it.

Polskaya helped himself to an espresso from the machine in the hallway and crossed his fingers to the sound of hissing and wheezing as his cup was filled with caffeinated liquid.

———

"Is she awake?"

Detective Line Hansen looked questioningly at Polskaya while trying to keep a whiff of dignity in the face of the doctor who hopefully had given Olya the ability to walk again.

"I don't know. I was just about to go in to see her."

The doctor was just back at work and grumpy, but he tried to be polite. He could easily admit that he liked this Line, with her narrow blue eyes and blonde curly hair, better than her male colleagues. Something about her appearance and attitude made him feel that she didn't consider her time more important than his.

"If you wait here, I can tell you how she's feeling. She will need recovery for a few weeks."

Line Hanson nodded. "Of course. I understand."

Polskaya steeled himself as he put his hand on the doorknob. Memories of the operation that had gone wrong flooded back. Back then, when he entered the room, he saw that she was awake. But she didn't react to his voice. When he moved toward her bed, he discovered that her sparkling green eyes had a glassy tint. It was as if her soul had disappeared.

This time, he was not sure what had happened. Olya lay motionless, with the faint light from the window on her face. Her long, dark curls laid over her Latin face with big, full lips.

As he quietly approached, he reminded himself to ask where she got her looks from.

When he came up to her, her eyes grew wide as if she had been startled.

"Are they here? Are they coming for me?"

FEBRUARY 12, 2012: DAY

WHEN FRANK HANSEN CAME HOME TO THE APARTMENT IN Eirik Jarls Gate, Alexandra was nursing.

Stine drank the milk from Alexandra's big breasts just like Frank envisioned a hungry cub sucking honey from a bee hive would've done.

He sat in the chair above his wife and looked into her eyes. "You need to listen to what I have to say."

"Tell me."

Frank told her about the trip to see Anne Berit, then the visit to Martine Skog, and finally about the magazines on the way home. Alexandra was silent.

"I may have to go a couple more times to interview several women. But I hope you understand why."

She smiled. "Do what you must, my hero."

———

IN A ROOM at St. Olav's Hospital, Kurt Hammer awoke with a slightly less headache than usual and felt an urge to smoke so huge that it felt like an abyss was opened in him. He reached for a nicotine gum package on the nightstand and threw two chewing gums into his mouth. Then he reached for his phone and dialed Editor Karlsen.

"Kurt. How are you?"

"All right. Felicia came back yesterday with something to sleep on, so I'm not tired. Did you happen to read the draft I sent you?"

"Yes, I just finished reading through, actually. Very good so far, but you lack sources."

"I sent Frank out yesterday to obtain a source. I think it went well. Turns out Blekstad was a monster who raped at least on one occasion. And he tried to rape Olya, as far as I under-stand it."

"What about Jansrud?"

"He's worse. I've tried, but..."

"What?"

"It's as if he's surrounded by an invisible wall. He used sexual services once. I doubt it was a one-time event."

"Go on, Kurt. I know you can do it."

"Thanks. I'll do what I can." He hung up and put his cell back on the nightstand.

———

HARRY OLSEN, one of Trondheim's most seasoned police investigators, sat in interrogation room two and studied Erik Larsen. The guy had changed from the pictures in the police database, but not much. Even with buzz cut and Hawaiian t-shirt, the contours of his face and the empty stare revealed a person with a long criminal career.

"Can you explain to me how a security guard at Værnes, Stieg Homme, was discovered murdered in his office after you left it?" Olsen tried his best to hide the disdain he felt for Larsen.

"Self-defense."

Olsen choked on his coffee and it splashed on the interrogation table. The red lamp on the wall went dark when his foot slipped off the recording pedal under the table.

"What did you say?"

"Self-defense."

"Can you re-tell what happened?"

"He said he had to talk to me before I could travel. I came with him to the office, where he tried to chip me down. You can ask that journalist. He can confirm that I was injured."

"Why did you proceed to flee from the police?"

"Obviously I knew you wouldn't believe me. I've been behind bars before."

"You understand that prosecutors will have a hard time believing that story, right?"

Silence.

"Well, over to different matters. The guard probably took you to his office because we received a tip that a person resembling you was seen right next to Trondheim Torg just before it blew up. What do have you to say to that?"

"I'll say nothing more before I get an attorney."

"Well, do you have any idea who?"

"Tor Erling Staff."

Harry Olsen's eyes became wide. "That... will be taken into consideration. The interview ended at 5:05 p.m."

Two tall police officers came into the room and handcuffed Erik Larsen.

Olsen tore his fingers through his dark brown, curly hair, took a gulp of coffee, and reflected on the state of affairs. *Tor Erling Staff. Isn't he about seventy-five? The media will love it, if nothing else.*

He rose from his chair, walked out of interrogation room two and down the hallway to the commissioner's office, where he pounded on the door.

"Come in!" Commissioner John Voll sat behind his desk and looked over papers. "Oh, hey. It's you, Olsen?"

"Yes, it's me. We need to talk."

"Hm, well, just talk. I keep looking over budgets. All the events lately are about to kill us."

Olsen sighed. "Well, unfortunately I can't do anything about that. I just came to say that... well, Larsen purports to have killed in self-defense."

Voll looked up.

"And that... do you believe it?"

"Not exactly."

"Well, then let the prosecutors decide."

"There is one thing. He wants Staff to defend him."

"Staff?"

"Tor Erling Staff."

Voll rolled his eyes.

"Lord, have mercy on us."

"I know. The media will be on us like vultures. I was wondering if I should start by calling the chief public prosecutor and start planning a press conference."

"Hm. Sounds like a plan."

"Yes, and then I must bring that journalist from Under Dusken in for interrogation. Larsen alleges that he can confirm that he was already injured. But the damage..."

"What?"

"Nothing. I'll have to talk to him."

Voll nodded and went back to his papers, while Olsen got up and walked out. Once out in the hallway, he dialed Public Prosecutor Runar Bekkelund. After waiting for nearly a minute, he got an answer.

"Bekkelund!"

"Yeah, hey. Harry Olsen from Trøndelag Police here. As it turns out, the suspect, Erik Larsen, has asked for Tor Erling Staff as a lawyer. I was wondering if that was something you'd like to look into?"

"Staff? You are aware that he's going to run through you?"

"With all due respect, I'll make sure that won't happen."

"You sound confident. Well, I'll be in touch."

"Thanks. And you, no leakage, huh?"

"What do you take me for?"

"Sorry. It's just that we've become paranoid. The press has been on us like leeches."

"Hah. I hope you don't think that it's going to be any better now."

"I was afraid you'd say that."

———

A phone call and a few hours later, Culture Editor Mathias Kristensen had materialized in interrogation two. He had showered, but his red hair was still pointing in all directions. Except for a swollen lower lip, Olsen didn't notice any major damage after the collision with Erik Larsen.

"You're a tough bastard, huh?" Olsen said.

"Well, it was good you showed up when you did. Otherwise, the situation could've been far worse."

"Erik Larsen is not a man to fuck with. The fact that you're not worse off than you are indicates that he may have incurred some damages. Can you remember if he was harmed after you tackled him?"

Mathias' gazed roamed the room. "I remember that he was bleeding."

"Do you remember where?"

"No, I don't, unfortunately. Maybe his upper body, but I didn't have time to register."

"Hm. Interesting. Do you think the damages may've had something to do with the crash?"

"Yes, that was my first thought. Should they have had anything to do with something else?"

"It... the police, we like to keep all possibilities open. But I've really gotten everything I needed from you. Thank you for coming in on such a short notice."

"My pleasure. I hope you have evidence enough to arrest him."

When Mathias Kristiansen had left interrogation two, Harry Olsen called the prison and ordered a full search and photography of all the injuries on Erik Larsen.

———

FRANK HANSEN WAS TIRED. He had spent most of the afternoon shopping around for a stroller, without finding anything that he or Alexandra could agree on. So he was now sitting on the black Landskrona sofa in the living room of their apartment in Eirik Jarlsgate, while Alexandra tried to put Stine to sleep.

When his phone rang, he took it from his pocket. Kurt.

"Hey, Kurt!"

"Hey, how did it go?"

"It went well. She even authorized me to talk to her doctor! I just haven't had time to send what I wrote yet."

"And Alex?"

"She took it well. She understands how important this is."

"That's good. I think I've found a source that may be relevant."

"Have you found anything on Jansrud?"

"I think I have."

"Fantastic. I'll take care of it. Just give me the address."

———

In a meeting at the Trondheim Police Station, the group responsible for the Blekstad and Jansru cases finally had time to meet. Around a table whose only decoration was a metal pot of coffee, Detective Superintendent Roy Dundre, Detective Line Hansen, as well as Detectives Martin Skaar and Brede Wiberg were seated.

"So," said Dundre, "the status quo is that the suspect, Olya Volkova, indirectly confessed to killing both men, but may only be linked forensically to the murder of Jansrud. We must, of course, act as if we have evidence for both murders when we get her in for questioning. Line, you've just been to the hospital. Can you update us?"

All eyes in the room fell on her. She wasn't big breasted, yet she was beautiful, with perfect facial features. In moments like this, she felt the full weight of working in a male-dominated environment.

"She was awake when I was there, but I didn't see her. The chief physician said she had experienced some kind of anxiety attack. He couldn't say if it was because of the surgery, but he expects it to pass. From my understanding, we could fetch her in a couple weeks."

Dundre thought for a while. "Well, let's hope she's physically and psychologically stable enough to be questioned by then. As we all know, she was at the Trondheim hotel when it was blown to smithereens by the madman. Martin and Brede, did you find any correlation between the cases?"

"Unfortunately, no."

Martin and Brede seemed, at least from a distance, like twins. Martin had black hair and Brede was blond, but they were the same age, spent a lot of time in the gym every day, and both had a penchant for gray Armani suits when they weren't in uniform. Both had graduated from the police college in Bodø that year and entered the Criminal department after only five years of service.

"Olsen says that the madman refuses to say a word without a lawyer," Dundre said. "He's supposed to be hosting a press conference tonight. Let's hope that the he'll manage to get something sensible out of the guy with a lawyer present."

———

Frank Hansen had to ease his conscience. After he started working on Kurt's story, he was still wasn't sure whether Olya had the right to do what she'd done, but he felt surer than ever that it had been wrong of him to surrender her to the police.

With a lump in his stomach, he called from the car, outside Eirik Jarls Gate.

"Kurt, I..."

"What?"

"I was the one who tipped off the police about Olya. Sorry."

"I thought as much. I'm not the one you should be apologizing to. Although, they probably would've discovered it sooner or later."

"All right, I get the point. I'll swing by the hospital before I go meet your source.

"Do that. And send me everything you have as soon as you've finished your interview."

Frank hung up and drove to St. Olav's Hospital. Inside the ER, things had calmed down after the bomb under Trondheim Torg. Doctors and nurses no longer ran around the hallways, but there were still plenty of patients in the halls, connected to heart monitors and drip machines which were rolled out for the occasion.

On NRK, political commentator Lars Nehru Sand and anchorwoman Ingerid Stenvold were discussing rumors about whether the arrest of a motorcyclist in Trondheim could have any connection with the press conference which had been announced that evening, and if the assassin had political motives, like Anders Behring Breivik.

When Frank knocked on Olya's door, he first received no answer. He knocked again, and a tired voice said, "Come in." He carefully opened the door and went in. Olya's verdigris eyes pierced him, as if they were looking into the depths of his soul.

"May I sit?"

"Please."

"Thanks. I'm—"

"I know who you are. Kurt told me."

"I'm the one who gave you up to the police. I've since realized that what I did was wrong."

"They deserved to die," she replied, without looking at him.

"I... I've thought a lot about that, and I'm still not sure I agree. But I know Blekstad was a monster, and I'm about to go see someone who Kurt believes was raped by Jansrud."

"Tell her he can't hurt her again."

"I will. I'm going to see Kurt before I leave. Anything you want me to say?"

"Tell him they're coming for me soon. And say thank you."

Frank nodded and stood to leave Olya's room.

───────

INSIDE KURT'S ROOM, Frank found him chewing on nicotine gum and reading on his iPad.

"Hi."

"Hi. What did she say?"

"She said they're coming for her soon, and that I should say thank you."

"Well, if this won't story get her out of jail, it'll certainly change people's perception." Kurt smirked and scratched his beard. "I just got done talking with Karlsen. I persuaded him to clear the front page on the day before the trial starts, if nothing else emerges.

"Good work. Frank sat beside the bed. Have they said anything about when you can get out of here?"

"About a month, he reckoned. But I have to start training my leg soon. And that's good. Otherwise, I'd go mad."

Frank smiled.

"That, I understand. I'm going off now to give you more to write. It was Upper Møllenberg 41, right?"

"Right you are!"

Fifteen minutes later, Frank Hansen's Passat swung onto the gravel square in front of Upper Møllenberg 41. The house stood out in the area, as it was the only thing that looked new among a plethora of older wooden houses. It was painted cream yellow and had a white staircase that lead to a brown door.

Frank jumped out of the car and hurried to the door, in the pouring rain. What met him when the door opened, shocked him. The woman inside wasn't as much a woman as a goddess. She had to be at least one meter seventy-eight, with long blonde hair that reached her to her perfect waist. The eyes that met his were almond shaped and dark brown. Her lips were thick and she had sandy white teeth.

"Skavlan. Rachel Skavlan." She stretched out a hand with perfect almond shaped nails.

"Hi. Frank Hansen here, from Aftenbladet. Can I come in?"

"Of course." She smiled and led him into a tiny outer

corridor with purple carpet and a row of hangers along one short wall.

Frank hung up his wet gray overcoat.

Within the hallway, there was another hallway with a staircase leading up to the second floor, and a door leading to a living room with an open kitchen.

"Coffee?" Rachel indicated that he sit on the black sofa in front of a flat-screen TV along a wall.

"Certainly." Frank sat and took out his notebook. "You were once Jansrud's girlfriend?

She came to him with an oblong coffee pot in shiny metal. "Don't you read tabloids?"

Frank did his best not to laugh. "I've been an employee at Trøndelag's largest newspaper for years, and I've never written a celebrity story in my life. So... no." He smiled.

"Well, when I broke up with him, it was on the front page of all the tabloids in the country."

Excuse me for saying so, but I guess he didn't take it well?"

She poured the boiling coffee into a white mug on the table in front of the couch. Then she put the jug on the table, sat and took a sip from her cup.

"He came here on a night much like today. It was stormy outside. He had been drinking. He does that a lot, off season. That's also been written about a lot."

"I'm not much interested in sports." Frank tried to look apologetic.

"Excuse me, but you aren't the one who's writing this story, are you?"

"Kurt Hammer, the guy you talked to, is in the hospital. He survived Trondheim Torg, barely. He's always been convinced that Jansrud's murder was self-defense, and he has convinced me."

Rachel thought about it and nodded.

Frank suspected that she really didn't like the idea of dealing with a journalist who didn't know who she was, but that he had managed to convince her that his intentions were good.

"I shouldn't have let him in, of course. First, he threw himself around me and begged me to take him back. I tried to comfort him, but when it became clear that I wasn't going to take change my mind, he snapped. I knew..." She put her face in her hands.

"Take the time you need," Frank said, calmly.

"It's all right," she said, after a while. "I knew he was combustible when drunk, but not in this way. He started calling me names and beating me. He broke my nose broke! I fainted, and when I woke up, I was tied up in my bed. I didn't understand how that was possible, as he had always been a meek man in bed. Now it was as if he was a completely different man. When he entered the room, evil protruded from his eyes. He held up a black dildo, and then it dawned on me how stupid I'd been."

Frank shuddered.

"You didn't know..."

"He drove the dildo into me, and I screamed so hard I thought my lungs would puncture."

"You said he broke your nose. I expect that you've been to a doctor?"

"Yes."

Frank looked at her as she stood and disappeared out of the room. Not long afterward, she was back with some papers and she lay them on the table in front of him. He looked at them and realized they were nasal X-rays.

"Take them," she said. "Copies."

"Thank you. May we print these?"

"Of course."

"This will really be helpful for our story. Thanks. Sorry I have to ask, but you didn't sustain any other injuries?"

"A severe sleep problem, and it hurts when I go to the bathroom. But mostly the latter. I can't sleep without having a girlfriend over."

"Did you go to the police?"

"I did, but the matter was dismissed."

———

FRANK CURSED to himself and backed out of the gravel driveway in front of Upper Møllenberg 41. He zoomed towards Midtbyen Medical center, Olav Tryggvason, gate 40.

As a journalist, it shouldn't have to be his responsibility to deal with matters that the police don't have the capacity for or wouldn't look into. But since that was the case, he would make sure they were dealt with properly.

Midtbyen Medical Center was next to O'Leary's restaurant, a reddish brown brick building with green shutters in front of large window facades. The medical center was a plain, dark and concrete building.

Frank was surprised when he was greeted by a man, who introduced himself as Hans Bergmann. Once inside the office, Frank pulled out a handwritten authorization from Rachel, which meant all his questions could be answered.

Bergmann read the proxy. "I guess you want to hear my professional opinion regarding the broken nose and the sex toy?" He looked at Frank with crystal blue eyes that contrasted a black crew cut over a face with broad jaws.

Frank nodded.

"Well, after studying radiographs, it's difficult for me to understand how the injury could have occurred by accident. Most likely, she was beaten or hit by an object the size of a fist.

When it comes to her feeling pain when she goes to the bathroom, the survey I undertook is consistent with violent penetration. It is simply not possible to—"

"Incur that type of injury with a sexual partner who exercises caution?"

"Exactly. Have you spoken to others?"

"Believe me, I have. Do you mind being quoted in the article?"

"No. As long as it's okay for Rachel.

Frank shook his hand and stood.

"Thank you for taking this time."

"Thank you for writing about a topic that the police aren't dealing with."

The two strangers gave each other a quick hug before Frank left the office.

———

A 9:59 P.M., Kurt Hammer received an email from Frank Hansen. Ten minutes later, he started writing.

FEBRUARY 10, 2012

WHEN OLEG ABAKUMOV'S DAUGHTER CAME INTO THE world, he was happier than ever before. Her eyes were pinched closed, and she had the same aquiline nose as her father.

The tall, slightly hunched man who would've been two meters with a straight back, lifted her little body with his strong hands and swung her around in the air.

"You'll be called Anastasia." A tear ran down his powerful cheekbones.

"She's hungry," said Anna. "Give her to me." She lay exhausted in bed at the European Medical Center in Spiridonyevski Street Five, Moscow, and looked at her overjoyed husband with tired eyes.

He walked toward his wife and placed Anastasia in the arms of her black-haired mother. Anna gazed tenderly at him with her green eyes received her daughter into to her chest.

"After her grandmother?" she asked.

"After her grandmother," he replied.

LATER, when they arrived at the three-room apartment in the dilapidated Yugo Zapadnaya region of Moscow, inside his Lada Nova, Anna looked at her husband and sighed. The red lipstick on her big lips were in stark contrast to the gray interior of the car with fragile windows.

"I'm afraid," she said.

He looked at her, bewildered. Even with fake fur, she looked confident and strong, more Italian than Russian, with her shoulder-length jet-black hair which encapsulated a round head above two large breasts.

"For what?" he asked.

"I love you, but we can't continue like this. You have no job, and now we have a daughter to support."

He had been a store manager for a shopping center and had been responsible for over fifty employees. On the day he was dismissed, after the center was bought out by some faceless organization, he'd learned that she was pregnant.

"It's going to be okay," he had said, and he repeated those words now.

She sighed again and opened the door to step out of the car. She continued across the littered lawn, toward entrance 14C without looking back.

All entrances looked the same and consisted of a gray metal door with numbers. Other than that, the facades contained no information about who lived where, making them about as ambiguous as her mandate to find a solution to the problem.

Oleg glanced at his watch. Quarter past four. *Igor Vasilev to be up by now.*

Fifteen minutes later, he parked his grayish-white Lada Nova in front of a ramshackle wooden building painted yellowish-green. The lot and the house must've looked impressive thirty to forty years ago. Now, the plot was overgrown with grass and dominated by a giant oak tree that had grown in such a way that it was impossible to see where the house began and the tree stopped.

Before he stepped out of the car, Oleg took a quick look in the mirror. He had close-cropped brown hair on top of a round face, brown eyes, and a stubble beard that covered most of the lower part of his face. He appeared tired, but he'd just have to ignore that for now.

He cautiously walked toward the entrance. One false step and he risked stepping on broken vodka bottles or syringes hidden in the grass. The blue wooden door creaked as he put his hand on the rusted door handle and pulled it toward him.

"Hello?"

If the outside of the house mirrored Igor's exterior, the inside mirrored his soul. The hallway was covered with stained wood and blue wallpaper, and even though the floor was crooked, there wasn't a speck of dust. The clothes, mostly leather, hung in a row.

"We're in here." a voice called, from the dining room.

Oleg took off his fake Nike shoes, put them on the shoe rack, and went into the dining room.

Igor Vasilev was a big man. He usually towered a foot or two above everyone he encountered. With his shaved head and always with a Cuban cigar in his mouth, he had a look that commanded respect. Right now, he sat with his back to the hallway and was getting massaged by one of his young lovers, who followed him like a tail wherever he went.

Oleg couldn't help staring at the ass of the blonde woman who couldn't have been older than twenty-five.

"Irya, forgive us. We need to talk man to man," Igor said.

The blonde turned and left them immediately. Oleg stared down at the floor, for fear of meeting her eyes.

"Come, my friend. Sit!"

Oleg went to him and sat on the other side of a rustic stained-wood dining table.

"What can I do for you?" Igor took a thorough puff of the Cuban and brought it out of his mouth with a grandiose movement.

"I'm broke and I just fathered a daughter. I need a job. Anything."

Igor smiled.

"Congratulations, old friend. Congratulations. Unfortunately, I don't have much right now. Come to think about it, you hunted with your father a lot, didn't you?"

"Yes. I still go hunting in the fall and winter."

"Ah, good. It turns out..." Another puff of the cigar. His head disappeared and all that could be seen through the smoke was the second-hand pinstriped suit and the purple handkerchief in his breast pocket. "... that I have a problem you can help me with. A priest at the Christ the Savior Cathedral has made it his mission to convert many of my colleagues. I have no vendetta against God." He put a cross of gold that hung around his neck up to his mouth and kissed it. "But if my colleagues don't perform their jobs, then it becomes a problem. If you help make the priest disappear, I will reward you greatly. Call it a win-win situation."

Oleg sighed. He had envisioned many things, but not this.

He clenched the cross he was carrying in his pocket. "I... give me some time to think about it."

"Of course. But don't think too long. I don't want your daughter to starve to death."

Oleg bowed and walked to the car, empty-handed. *Can I go home? No. I should go and talk to my priest.*

Ten minutes later, he parked in front of the Church to the

Intercession of Fili, on Novozavodskaya Street. The church reminded him of a pyramid, how it stretched towards the sky, with six floors, adorned with small onion-shaped domes of gold. Many of his friends found it ugly because it was brick. But Oleg loved it. For him, it was the finest of all the churches throughout Moscow. Here, he was baptized. Here, he had come to know God.

His priest was at work. Father Aleksandr was bent in prayer before the altar of gold, flanked by a relief depicting Jesus's last meal with his disciples. When he finally stood, rays of sunshine dropped through the church window and made his red bucket hat seem like a ruby that contrasted his black robe.

"Oleg, my son. What brings you to these parts, outside mass?"

"I need to talk, Father."

"Confess or just talk?"

"It's not something I've done, but something I'm about to do."

"Let's sit in the sunshine outside."

"All right, Father."

The old priest took several minutes to walk out of the church. When he finally got outside and sat on one of the red-painted benches outside, Oleg wondered whether he had proposed to go outside just to see if he was still able to incur such a physical strain on his body. Aleksandr's gray beard reached him down to his feet when he sat.

"So, my son, what was it you wanted to talk to me about?"

"If you had the choice between belittling God or watching the ones you loved most wither away, what would you do?"

"My son, sometimes God asks that we face brutal choices. Often, it is to test the strength of our faith."

"So you think I should put my beloved's lives at stake over blind faith?"

"It is written in Genesis, chapter twenty-two, God said, *'Take your son, your firstborn, and go to the Moria region. Sacrifice him there on a mountain I will show you.'* Early the next morning, Abraham got up and loaded his donkey. He took with him two servants and his son Isaac. When he had cut enough wood for the burnt offering, he set off to the place God had told him about. On the third day, Abraham looked up and saw the place in the distance. He said to his servants, *'Stay here with the donkey while I and Isaac go over there. We will pray, then come back to you.'* Abraham took the wood for the sacrifice and gave it to his son Isaac, while he himself bore fire and the knife. While the two walked together, Isaac said to his father, *'Father?'*

'Yes, my son,' replied Abraham.

'The wood and fire is here,' Isaac said, *'but where is the lamb for the sacrifice?'*

'God himself will provide the lamb for the sacrifice, son,' said Abraham.

When they reached the place God had told about, Abraham built an altar there and laid the wood on top. He tied up his son Isaac and laid him on the altar, on top of the wood. Then he took out the knife to slay his son. An angel of the Lord called out to him from heaven, *'Abraham! Abraham!'*

'Here I am,' he replied.

'Do not put a hand on him,' said the angel. *'Do not do anything with him. Now I know that you fear God, because you have not withheld your firstborn.'*

God will always provide for you and yours if you are faithful."

Oleg shook his head. "Then God better accept my apology for what I'm about to do."

He kissed Aleksandr on the cheek, got up and strode to the car.

When he returned, Igor was sitting with his feet on a stool and looking out of living room window, which was almost entirely covered by roots. He sucked on a new cigar. On the coffee table was a cell phone.

"I'm doing it."

"I knew you would." Igor pointed to the phone. "Take it. It's a Blackphone. I'll send you the details."

Oleg took it, gave his old friend a kiss on the cheek, and headed back to the car. He drove back to the apartment, more determined than he'd been in a long time.

The black elevator with steel lattice rattled and rumbled as it slowly brought him up to the eighth floor.

What I've been asked to do is terrible. But maybe we could move to a place more suited to raising a child. God can't give us protection or an income. Not here. Oleg had lost several close friends to overdoses, violence, abuse, and cold. *In Russia, every poor soul must provide for themselves.*

"Hello?" he called.

No one answered. He took off his shoes and put them into the cheap shelf made out of imitated mahogany, which was under a mirror in the small hallway that connected the rooms in the apartment. The hall was covered with orange carpet with brown triangles in the middle. Oleg hated it but couldn't afford to replace it.

Anna sat in the kitchen. She drank black tea, fed Anastasia, and had a newspaper spread out in front of her on the small plastic table. It was situated along one short wall of their kitchen, which was just big enough for two adults.

"Are you coming with money?" She didn't look up.

"I'm coming with harbingers of better times."

He sat in front of her on the vacant plastic black stool on the other side of the table.

"What have you done now?"

"It's not what I've done. It's what I'm about to do. You love me no matter what, right?"

"In Russia, every person is responsible for their own destiny. We can't live only on air and love."

"I know, dear, I know." He got up and walked around the table to kiss her.

———

THE NEXT MORNING, he woke up at four forty-five to the sound of a message ticking in on his Blackphone.

Sergei Ilyavitsj Blok.

The name was followed by a picture. The priest looked like a younger version of Father Aleksandr, with a jet-black beard, red bucket hat, and eyes black as coal. High cheekbones made him look elegant.

Oleg assumed he had to be at work or on the way there, since he got the message now.

Fortunately, Anna hadn't noticed anything. If he was quick, he could return before she got up.

He stopped by the kitchen on his way out and picked up kitchen gloves and a stainless steel knife. For a moment, he considered taking his Mosin-Nagant M91/30 PU Sniper, which he had inherited from his father, but then realized he wouldn't have time to find a suitable place to shoot from. It'd have to wait until next time.

Outside, it was raining cats and dogs, so he hurried to his car parked on the sidewalk. He had on a black coat with a large collar, and a brown fedora, and hoped it would be enough to hide him if spotted.

Ten minutes later, he parked outside Yogozapadny Subway. The white concrete building was probably one of the dullest stations on the Sokolnicheskaya line, and Oleg envisioned that Ya Tatarzhinskaya couldn't have been paid much to design the station in the sixties.

He ran across the street, and five minutes later he stood eight meters below ground, between two rows of white concrete columns. The entire station was empty except for a couple of suited men with briefcases, apparently on their way to work.

Soon, he stood in Volkonka Street and followed the street lights and the big gilded onion-shaped dome all the way to no. fifteen. He glanced at the Blackphone. The display showed 5:45. The large avenue leading to the church was practically empty except for a few priests and some pious apparently about to attend to morning mass.

Oleg sat on one of the brown benches along the avenue. He looked at the picture of Sergei again. How would he find him?

He decided to walk slowly towards the church while taking a thorough look at the priests he passed.

Wait, what was that? A taxi? Could it be... no. Gray beard, too old. Here's one with a bent nose. There, a blue-eyed one. None looked like the man in the picture.

Finally, he decided to go around the entire whitewashed building before he entered. *Yes, it's nice. But it's a pity that it's often the only church tourists get to see when they come to Moscow.*

Eventually, Oleg found his target sitting alone in the rain, on a bench behind the huge church. He calmly walked over and sat beside him. The black beard reminded him of wet wool, and it extended down to on the stomach of the young priest.

"Why are you sitting out here in the rain alone, Father?"

"God created rain so that it would give life to everything on Earth. Why shouldn't I enjoy it?"

"You're not properly dressed, Father. You can get sick. Here, let me help you."

Oleg slipped the kitchen knife out of his coat pocket and into the side of the priest, who groaned and slumped down. He was about to rise, and Oleg wrapped his arms around him to hold him down, and drove the knife into his heart. His hands were blood-red, and he cursed himself for forgetting to put on the kitchen gloves.

He had to remain calm. He took out his cross, kissed it, laid it on the priest's forehead and did the sign of the cross over his own chest.

"In the name of the Father, the Son, and the Holy Spirit, forgive me for this sin," he whispered. "Amen."

Oleg grabbed the priest's hand and cut off two fingers. He packed them a kitchen glove and put it in his coat pocket.

———

A copper colored KamAZ 6560 trailer crawled up and stopped in front of the wooden ramshackle house that belonged to Igor Vasilev. Out of the car came two men in their mid-thirties, both with tattooed arms, one dressed in jeans and a military jacket over a blue polo shirt, the other wearing a brown leather jacket over an Adidas tracksuit. Both had on black military boots and strode straight to the house.

Inside the living room, Igor Vasilev sat cross-legged on a mat on the floor, listening to Indian music from speakers mounted in the corners. He was dressed in a blue tracksuit and had a Cuban in his mouth.

"Ah, you're back," he said, when the two men entered his living room.

"Yes, it's good to be back in the motherland," said the man in the leather jacket, who was the tallest of the two.

"Do you have anything to report?"

"Well, everything went as planned. But when we reached the Finland border we heard rumors."

"Rumors?"

"Yes, that things didn't go as planned. The operation... they had a mole in their midst, and he went berserk. He almost killed them all, and those who weren't killed were arrested."

"Hm. Interesting. The rumors reached me, too." An oily smile spread across Igor's fat lips. "I just wanted to hear you say it."

"We couldn't help it. It happened after we were gone."

"Well, now we have a problem, haven't we?"

The two men looked at each other. "Yes, we have."

"Fortunately, I've decided that I'll take care of it."

"Really?"

"Really. After all, it wasn't your fault. But don't make fools of yourselves again. Where are the others?"

"They've already gone to fetch more."

"Very well. You can go and help."

Just as the two men turned to go back to the hallway they'd came from, they were hit in the back of the head. They collapsed and landed on top of another, lifeless as a couple potato sacks.

———

BACK IN THE APARTMENT, Anna hadn't yet risen. A sleepy silence covered the apartment like a veil, as if time had stood still while he was away.

He tiptoed into the kitchen, removed the kitchen gloves from his pocket, and placed them on the kitchen table. Then he took out the bloody fingers and laid them on the gloves before photographing them with the Blackphone. He sent the picture to the number he'd received the message from. Then he took the fingers to the bathroom and flushed them down the toilet. *I'll be damned if I retain evidence.*

He washed his hands in the small, round porcelain sink in front of the mirror. The water was red, and the unmistakable smell of iron entered his nostrils.

Finally, he went back to the kitchen, grabbed the kitchen gloves, took them to the bathroom and cut them into strips with a knife. Then he flushed the toilet again.

He went back into the hallway and took off his coat before going to the bedroom, where he made sure to put the clothes exactly as they had been before he got up. Finally, he laid back in the double bed and fell asleep almost immediately.

———

HE WOKE up to a kiss on the cheek from Anna.

"Sorry I've been angry, but I worry for Anastasia's future."

"You needn't worry any more. I have secured her future."

"What have you done?"

"It doesn't matter. We need not worry anymore."

Oleg noticed that he had received a new message on his Blackphone. He picked it up from the nightstand.

Well done. Check your account.

"Stay here," he said. "I'm going out to buy breakfast for us."

Outside the local Lenta shop, he checked his balance on an old, battered ATM. His eyes became wet as he realized that his family wouldn't have to worry about money for the next six months.

In the store, he grabbed a bottle of Chianti Classico to celebrate, and then stood in line checkout line. *I've done what I had to do to save my family. Are our lives worth less than that of the priest's?* He looked at the ceiling and did the sign of the cross on his chest.

After entering his home, a new message appeared on his cell phone.

You must go to Norway. Plane leaves tomorrow. Ticket info is attached. You'll get more information when you land.

When Anna came into the kitchen, Oleg had made toast, scrambled eggs, tea, and had opened the Chianti.

"Where is Anastasia?" he asked.

"She sleeps, vozlyublennyy. How did you get to afford all this? You haven't done anything... for him?"

Oleg sat with a sigh. "I had no choice, vozlyublennyy."

Anastasia sat on the other side of the table, took a few leaves of tea into a cup, poured in hot water, and drank a few sips.

"As long as you don't tell me what you do."

"I need to travel to Norway tomorrow."

She gave him a stunned look. "To Norway! Are you going to leave us?"

"I promise to come back after a week."

"You promise?"

"I promise."

He walked over to her and gave her a passionate kiss.

———

WHEN OLEG HAD TAKEN up position in a silent cabin on the NSB train from Værnes Airport, at 11:05 p.m., his Blackphone vibrated in his pocket. He took it out and saw a picture of a man with shoulder-length, shaggy hair, who wore a fedora and had a cigarette hanging out of his mouth. Oleg thought he resembled an American actor he'd seen in a movie about a guy who had his rug stolen and was mistaken for a millionaire.

Name: Kurt Hammer. Location: St. Olav's Hospital, it said underneath the picture.

Oleg shuddered. If the guy was hospitalized, the mission would almost be too easy.

A quick search on the web revealed that the St. Olav hotel was nearest to the hospital. *No one will suspect that the killer's staying right next to the hospital.*

Upon exiting Trondheim Central Station, he got a taxi and said, in clumsy Norwegian "Mauritz Hansens, gate 3."

"You got it," said the driver, who looked Indian or Pakistani, with chocolate skin, jet black hair slicked back, and a big beard. "Are you visiting someone in the hospital?"

"Huh? Я не говорю по-норвежски." *I don't speak Norwegian.*

The driver looked at him, suspiciously. "Are you going to visit someone in the hospital," he asked, in English, with his local Trønder dialect.

Silence.

"Indeed. He's... old friend."

The first thing Oleg noticed about Trondheim was the traffic. *In Moscow, there are traffic jams all the time. Here, it flows.* In addition, the houses were remarkably low. There were no skyscrapers, as far as he could see. The facades there were pristine. There weren't dilapidated facades on every street corner, like in Russia. Most people seemed to wear expensive clothes. *I'm definitely not at home.*

"Welcome to Norway." The driver parked in front of what looked like a large apartment complex, painted white on a red background, and had large window facades.

"Thank you. I will need it." Oleg stepped out of the car, into the pouring rain.

The first thing he passed on the way into the reception was an abstract painting by the artist Pramila Giri. As far as he could understand, it consisted of nothing else than a red, an orange, a purple, and a blue stripe on a dark blue background.

133

He had never understood abstract art, but the colors matched the ones on the whitewashed wall of the outer corridors here. The reception was decorated like a living room, complete with a fireplace, a flat-screen TV, and a sofa. Along one window stood two green designer chairs on either side of a table lamp and a small potted plant.

Inside the reception, Oleg shuddered because the taxi bill cost as much as half the average weekly salary in Russia. He didn't look forward to finding out what the hotel bill would cost.

He booked room on the top floor. It turned out to be sparsely decorated, with a double bed, two green armchairs, a flat-screen TV and light brown curtains. The TV was the only thing that really impressed him, but he didn't care all that much. He wouldn't get to spend much time there, anyway.

He left his briefcase with a few clothes and his Mosin-Nagant M91/30 PU Sniper beside the bed and took a refreshing shower. Then he decided to brave the rain for some reconnaissance.

Other than a church building with a tall spire, he couldn't recall having seen any tall buildings from the taxi. Downstairs, in the reception area, he checked his Blackphone, and it turned out that the tallest building in Trondheim, apart from the church, was the Scandic Lerkendal hotel, which was a short walk away.

Fifteen minutes later, he passed the local football stadium—remarkably small—and stood in front of a seventy-five-meters-high whitewashed building with dark windows that reminded him of pieces in a famous Russian game, Tetris, which he had played in elementary school.

Then he fished out his Blackphone from his coat pocket and typed a message.

Book a room at the Scandic Lerkendal hotel in Trondheim, top floor.

An hour later, he found himself in front of Bakke Church on Solsiden, in Trondheim. The red-painted church with caramel colored moldings and bright green spires housed Trondheim's only Russian Orthodox church. The church was empty except for a lone priest who sat on the first row of benches.

"Good day. Are you Father Dima?"

"Yes, that's right. And you must be Oleg?"

"Right."

"Have you come to confess?"

Dima looked at him with a pair of intense blue eyes under a lilac hat. He had a reddish beard that reached down on his stomach.

"In a way, yes."

"What's troubling you, my son?"

"I killed a son of God. Not only a son of God, but one of his faithful servants. I was desperate and did it to save my wife and daughter."

"My son, there are some things even the Almighty God can't forgive. Not without remorse and sacrifice."

"I regret that I have let myself be used as a weapon, out of the greed in my heart. And I regret that I must do it again."

Dima sighed. "You can still turn. Even in the valley of the shadow of death, there is always light. If you truly repent, you will turn, because you realize that the path you're walking is dark and cold.

"Sorry, Father, but if I give up now, I'm a dead man."

"So sacrifice yourself for what you believe in."

"Does it matter to God who dies?"

"What matters is what you do with the time you have been given on Earth.

"I will use my time to survive."

Oleg pulled his coat tighter around himself as he left the church and entered the pouring rain. After he arrived back to Hotel St. Olav, he received a new message.

Room booked for two nights. No. 719. You're checked in as Incognito.

Of all the things Kurt Hammer could've expected to wake up to the next day, a kiss on his cheek from Felicia wasn't on the list.

"Kurt, I read through the story. It's amazing!"

"Thanks. I'm quite excited myself, but Frank did the grunt work."

"I sent him a message."

———

Oleg had got up early that day. After much back and forth the night before, he had reached the conclusion that it would be too risky to ask for Kurt Hammer's room number. So he got up at seven, put on a cowboy hat he'd purchased at the airport, and pulled it tight over his forehead before he went to the reception desk at St. Olav's Hospital.

The fat lady in her forties, with a bowl cut had probably been so desensitized from the recent terrorist attack in Trondheim—which Oleg hadn't been able to avoid hearing about on all the news channels during the past week— that she didn't even bat an eye when he asked for the emergency ward, but only waved him in the direction.

Around nine o'clock, he arrived at the Scandic Lerkendal, room 719. The first thing he did was put his Blackphone at full volume. Then he set it to play Schubert's Ellens Gesang III, opus 56, no. 6, on repeat.

When that was done he unpacked all the twenty-four parts of his sniper rifle and mounted them consecutively. Last, he attached part twenty-five—his homemade silencer.

At 11:23, he had located Kurt Hammer's room. Much to his chagrin, Hammer had a visitor.

Oleg kissed the cross around his neck, tightened his grip on the gun and pulled the trigger.

———

KURT HAMMER HAD EXPERIENCED several shooting incidents in his life. But he had never been shot at from such a distance that he had no idea where the shots came from.

Nevertheless, when Felicia cried out, he immediately knew that she'd been shot. He grabbed her neck with both hands and pulled her close.

"You've been shot. Lay still!"

She opened her mouth to speak, but before she could utter a word, he tongue-kissed her while hoping that another shot wouldn't be fired.

———

OLEG HELD HIS BREATH. *Did I hit him?*

There was no movement down there.

He shot again.

KURT COULD FEEL Felicia's body shake after she was hit again. This time, the window smashed and pieces of glass flew in all directions. He pulled her closer to him as shards drilled into his skin.

THIRTY SECONDS.

One minute. Still no movement.

Oleg put down the gun and began to remove the silencer.

AFTER WHAT FELT LIKE AN ETERNITY, Kurt lifted his arm and pulled the rope over his head. A red light shone on the wall in front of him and indicated that help was on the way.

"Felicia! Are you alive? Where were you hit?"

She barely nodded. "In the shoulder, twice, I think." Her voice was thin and lifeless.

The first person to enter the room was nurse Viktoria. One look at Felicia and she ran over to see two gaping holes in her left shoulder. When she noticed that Kurt's hand was covered with glass, she turned around and saw the broken window.

"Oh, my God! What happened?"

"She's been shot," Kurt said. "Get her to the operating room, right away!

Just as Anna had managed to support Felicia's over the threshold, Officers Marie and Robert hurried into the room.

"Lord. What?"

"What does it look like?" Kurt yelled. "Where were you?"

"The two officers looked at each other, with terrified expressions.

Robert was in the bathroom, and I heard nothing."

"Well, it was a good thing you weren't here, otherwise he wouldn't have thought we were in danger."

Robert turned in the doorway, with impressive ease for a stocky man of two meters.

"What was he doing?" Kurt asked Officer Marie.

"Presumably making sure you get a new room. One that it's possible to listen in on."

Kurt knew it was useless to protest, so he turned his back, displaying the broken glass etched into his cut skin, and waved her away.

"Holy shit! I'll get someone to come take a look at you."

———

OLEG HADN'T YET LEFT his room at the Scandic Lerkendal hotel when he heard sirens near St. Olav's Hospital and realized that his precious rifle had to stay in Norway if he wanted any chance of getting home. On the way back to the St. Olav hotel, he dumped his briefcase in a trash can along the sidewalk.

———

"OUT, out. This is a crime scene, now!"

Detective Inspector Roy Dundre entered the room with flailing arms.

Kurt looked at him with wide eyes. "Is that always how you treat crime victims?"

Dundre shot him a disapproving glance. "What's happening?"

"As you can see, nurse Viktoria here is removing shards of glass from my body. If you want my theory—you probably don't, but you'll get it anyhow—then there aren't many places the shooter could've been located. I'm guessing the office building at Gløshaugen or the Scandic Lerkendal hotel."

Dundre walked out without saying a word.

Five minutes later, he came back and turned to nurse Viktoria. "Can I interview him while you're doing that?"

"By all means, I'm almost done."

"Did you send any people to those locations?" asked Kurt.

"No comment. I don't want you reporting what we're up to, in your idiotic newspaper. Can you tell me exactly what happened?"

Kurt paused. "I was awakened by Felicia. She came in and kissed me on the cheek and congratulated me on a story. She was here for probably twenty minutes, before she screamed out in pain. About a minute later, after I'd held her under me and told her that she should remain quiet, the glass shattered. She was hit in her shoulder twice, the way I understood it."

"You didn't hear a shot?"

"No. Not a damn thing. But there aren't any buildings in the vicinity that would've been possible to fire from. Couldn't have heard anything from Scandic or Gløshaugen."

"Do you think it's the same people that attempted to kill you outside Nidaros Cathedral?"

"Yes. Either them or the Russians."

"The Russians?"

"Yes. When five hundred kilos of heroin vanish without a trace, they must find someone to blame."

"Are you almost done here so he can get to another room," Dundre asked Anna.

"In about an hour or two. I'm afraid that some of these wounds need stitches."

"Shit." He left the room.

———

Doctor Polskaya knocked on Olya Volkova's door.

"Come in."

"How are you?" He approached, calm and controlled.

"They're here?"

He nodded.

"But I won't let them pick you up until I know whether or not you're able to walk, and until I feel certain that your mental health—"

"I'm not afraid of them anymore. They can't hurt me. Kurt and his friend are helping me."

Polskaya smiled. "Glad to know you're feeling better."

"Thank you. For everything."

"Just doing my job."

———

Line, Roy, Brede, and Martin were assembled again, in a meeting at the Trondheim Police Station. After five minutes of silence, in which everyone had alternately stared at the table and at each other, Roy Dundre spoke.

"I've sent people to scour the Scandic Lerkendal hotel and the office buildings at Gløshaugen for clues. Kurt was convinced the shooting had to have taken place from one of those places, and even though I hate to admit it, I think he may be right."

"How are the officers," asked Line.

"They're shocked, of course, but they... they may request some time off, in which case I'll find someone to replace them. Kurt has been moved to another room."

"What about the press conference tonight?" Brede said. "Should we be attending?"

Dundre shot him an angry glance. "Under *no* circumstances will this be spread to the media! We'll look helpless."

"Have you forgotten that Kurt is a journalist," asked Martin. "If he hasn't already called his editor, he'll surely do it within the day."

Roy sighed. "We may as well attend the press conference."

———

FRANK HANSEN WAS in the bathroom, changing his daughter's diaper, when his cell rang. He had placed it on the edge of the sink, next to him. As it was about to fall off, he threw a diaper in her face while trying to catch his phone.

"Damn, Kurt, this better be important." He pushed the answer button. "Hello?"

"Frank, this is Kurt. Someone tried to kill me. Just wanted you to hear it from me first."

"My God, Kurt, what happened? Are you all right?"

"Dunno exactly with me, but Felicia was shot twice in the shoulder. She's having surgery now."

"Is she going to survive?"

"I think so. She's being taken care of. I've called the editorial department, and someone's writing a story on it now. There's a press conference at the police station tonight. They'll most likely mention it there."

Frank sighed. "Are you wanting me to go since you can't?"

"Huh? No, I just figured you'd really want to know about it—"

"All right, I'll think about it. Thanks for letting me know."

"See ya."

———

KURT HUNG UP. "Hell, couldn't they have hit me instead of Felicia?" *Guess we're not supposed to be together again just yet, darling.*

He took out a bottle that Felicia had brought and took a sip. Then he cheered at the ceiling before laying down to sleep.

———

FRANK HANSEN STOOD in the kitchen of his apartment, on Eirik Jarl Street and called the chief editor of Aftenbladet, Harry Karlsen.

"Hey, boss."

"Frank!"

"Hey, I just wondered if you had someone to cover the press conference tonight. You see, Kurt called, and so—"

"I was actually about to call you. I know that you're on paternity leave, so I hesitated. But..."

Frank sighed. "I'll talk to my wife and then text you."

"Thank you, Frank."

Frank hung up to the sound of the wind howling outside and rain lashing against the windowpanes. He brought a large cup of coffee into the living room, where Alexandra was sitting.

"Can I attend a press conference tonight?"

"Is it about those assholes that were murdered?"

"Kurt was the victim of an attempted assassination."

"Huh? How so?"

"Someone shot at him, but they ended up hitting Felicia, a colleague. They're doing all right, but at the press conference the police will be talking about who they think was responsible."

Alexandra sighed. "Do you promise to come home early?"

"I promise." He leaned forward and kissed her forehead.

———

Frank sat in the front row of the audience, at the Trondheim Police Station and read Aftenbladet.no on his phone. The article, "Killer on the Loose in Trondheim", featured a short interview with Kurt Hammer, explaining the events. Finally, it said that Felicia Alvdal had been shot, but that she was going to survive.

The atmosphere was that of the calm before a storm. Most journalists were aware that the man who had killed a guard at Værnes had been apprehended, that he was probably a high-ranking member of the Hell's Angels, and that he was also involved in the drive-by at Nidaros Cathedral. But rumors were circulating about whether the police had made him confess, when his trial would eventually be held, and who he'd chosen as a lawyer.

When Criminal Inspector Harry Olsen entered the room, followed by Detective Inspector Roy Dundre, whispers were replaced by a shower of flashing camera lights.

Olsen looked tired. A protruding stomach was a testimony to many long days at work, and his full beard needed trimming. He wore a gray Armani suit that was a few sizes too small.

Inspector Dundre also had a protruding stomach, but it was smaller than his colleague's. He had a matching suit from Dressmann which fit him a little better. His walrus mustache was freshly trimmed, but his light blue eyes revealed fatigue from a heavy workload.

Harry Olsen got straight to the point. "Yesterday, around eleven o'clock, Erik Larsen was arrested outside Under Dusken's premises at Vollabakken, suspected of having knifed Stieg Homme to death. He is currently denying guilt but will be detained until further notice. We also have reason to believe... *ahem*... that Erik Larsen could be the one behind the attack on Trondheim Torg. A person matching his description was seen driving a motorcycle underneath Trondheim Torg right before it blew up. We are continually working to obtain evidence which will link him to the crime scene. Larsen has requested a lawyer, and attorney Tor Erling Staff has agreed to take the assignment. Now, I will turn the podium over to my colleague Roy Dundre."

"Thanks." Dundre coughed. "As some of you already know, an incident occurred at St. Olav's Hospital today. A journalist from Aftenbladet, Kurt Hammer, from what we understand, was nearly murdered as he lay in his hospital bed. His colleague, Felicia Alvdal, was shot and is currently undergoing surgery. When it is finished, we will hopefully know what kind of gun was used. We are doing our best to locate the perpetrator, but currently we don't have many clues. At this point, we are ready for questions."

A woman in her thirties, with shoulder-length red hair, stood.

"Frida Dalbakk from NRK, here. The story that was written by Aftenbladet mentions the possibility that a Russian was behind the assassination attempt on Hammer. What do you have to say about this?"

"We can neither confirm or deny that," Dundre said.

"So what you are saying is that someone from another country is now randomly killing people?"

Dundre looked as if he was about to explode, but he managed to keep his cool.

"Like I said, we can neither confirm or deny that. Next!"

Hansen stood. "Frank Hansen from Aftenbladet. Do you have a possible motive for killing Homme?"

"Like I said, Larsen hasn't admitted anything," Olson said.

"But we have reason to believe that he tried to leave the country when he was stopped by Homme. We've found electronic tickets to Amsterdam and Miami. Larsen has said that he was going on vacation to visit his children and grandchildren."

Klassekampen's blond emissary rose. "Jo Skårderud from Klassekampen. Is there any reason why the suspect has chosen Tor Erling Staff? And has Staff said why he took the assignment?"

"The suspect hasn't said anything on the matter," Olsen replied. "But we suspect that it's because he wants media attention. And Staff thought it was an interesting assignment."

———

Doctor Erlandsen looked at his watch. His brushed metal Lorus said it was 7:30.

"Maria, note the time. Both bullets have been found." He removed a 7.92 x 57mm Mauser bullet and dropped it in a metal bowl along with the first bullet."

"It's been noted."

"Good. I guess I just have to sow her together, here."

Fifteen minutes later, Erlandsen had removed his surgical gown and straightened his curly brown hair. Inside the office, he sent a message to Detective Inspector Roy Dundre.

Two bullets located. Patient in good condition. Contact me for handover of bullets. Erlandsen.

He had never been involved in a luckier case. She'd been millimeters from being an amputate.

He shook his head. *But it's probably best that she's kept in the dark.*

FEBRUARY 14, 2012

Oleg stood from his bed, at the St. Olav hotel, with a sinking feeling in his stomach. The police had appeared sooner than he'd expected yesterday. Now border crossings would be guarded, so his only option would be taking a train to Sweden.

After a hearty breakfast, where he noticed that the local newspaper had pictures of a press conference held by the police at the front, he went to reception and ordered a taxi to the train station.

The time was barely nine-thirty in the morning. Inside the hotel, it was completely quiet. But outside was seething with life. Cars came and went, and a helicopter took off with its distinctive sound—*swoosh, swoosh, swoosh.*

Oleg marveled. Maybe someone else had been killed by someone God had turned a blind eye to. Or maybe it was about to go to a traffic accident. Another fate left to itself by God's almighty hand. Maybe someone higher on the social ladder had decided to fight one of their wars over drugs or territories, as they did in the motherland.

"Sir?"

Oleg looked at the suit-clad man in reception.

"Your taxi is waiting, sir."

Oleg nodded as thanks and went out into the rain.

On the way to the train station, he sat stared out the window of the taxi. Despite the constant rain, he realized that he wouldn't mind living there. He couldn't quite put his finger on whether it was the expensive clothes people wore or the hotshot houses, but this country seemed safer than the one he came from.

When he exited at Trondheim Central Station, he proceeded to the platform. The train was due for departure in about ten minutes.

Down in the departure hall, which went up to the platform, there was a long line. Oleg extricated his passport from the inner pocket of his jacket and braced himself. *I'm going to get caught. But what have I got to lose?*

Arriving at the end of the queue, he was asked to show his passport by two police officers who looked like they were straight out of police college.

"Where are you going, sir?"

"Oslo?"

One officer looked him up and down with probing blue eyes. "I'm afraid you're going to have to come with me."

"I have to be on this train."

"We might be able to recoup your expenses, but we can't promise anything." The officer grabbed Oleg's arm and led him out of the line.

"Am I arrested, Officer?"

"No. But I'm retaining you for questioning."

———

INSIDE A LARGE INTERROGATION room with white walls, two tables, a lamp on the wall, and a couch along the same wall, Oleg was greeted by a middle-aged man with a powerful presence, bristling hair, and walrus mustache.

"Morning. My name is Roy Dundre. And you are?"

"Oleg."

The man pressed a pedal under the table, and the lamp on the wall was lit.

"Interview with suspect Oleg started at 10:45, on the 14th of April. Mr. Oleg, have you been to the Scandic Lerkendal hotel in the last few days."

"Yes. Is that a crime?"

"As it happens, my people recently discovered a briefcase thrown into a trash can in the vicinity. It contained a gun. A rifle, to be more specific. And not just any type of rifle, but a Russian Mosin-Nagant M91/30 PU Sniper. You wouldn't happen to know anything about that, would you?"

"This is an outrage. These are baseless accusations. I refuse to say another word without a lawyer."

"Very well. But first we need your fingerprints."

A policewoman materialized, with an ink casket. Oleg reluctantly brought his thumb up to the plate and placed it on the sheet that was put before him. Then he did the same for the next thumb before he was handcuffed by the blonde woman.

FELICIA WOKE up with a dull pain in her shoulder. A plastic tube was inserted into her hand and connected to a container of morphine.

Her mind was empty. *What the hell had happened?* She closed her eyes.

Out of the misty morphine porridge rose two memories—shots, Kurt Hammer.

She wound the medicinal tape off her hand and removed the stopper of plastic tubing. Then she jumped out of bed and rushed out of the room. In the hallway, she almost collided with a middle-aged man with chocolate brown almond eyes and curly brown hair.

"Ah, Felicia, how good to see you back on your feet. You can probably go home in a couple weeks. But if I were you, I'd go to back to bed. Morphine can make you a bit groggy."

"If I do, can you roll my bed to Kurt Hammer's room? He saved my life. I need to talk to him."

"Well, I suppose so."

———

"Who the fuck has been leaking information?

Roy Dundre's face was red as a tomato, and his temples revealed a blood vessel that looked as if it could burst any minute. He had summoned his colleagues for an emergency meeting.

"What's happening," asked Line.

"We have NCIS on our doorstep. Or, more accurately, we had. They're with him now. They insisted."

"Why would PST be interested in a Russian killer," asked Brede.

"I have no fucking clue, but I'm assuming it has something to do with the drug case that Kurt worked on for NCIS. I swear, if I find out that one of you leaked information, I'll personally make sure that you won't get close to a uniform for as long as you breathe!"

———

Oleg had barely sat in an isolation cell for a few hours, when the door was opened and two police officers came to fetch him.

"Where are we going?"

"You have some people waiting to talk to you."

Inside the interrogation room two sat two men in hats and gray coats. One had graying hair and a goatee. The other had fair hair and looked as if he was half as old as the other.

When Oleg came into the room, they stood and met him with awe in their eyes.

"Who are you?" Oleg asked.

"We're from the Norwegian FSB. Please sit." The elder man pointed toward the interrogation table."

"Do you have any idea what you've done?" the younger man said, once they were seated."

"I haven't done anything," Oleg said, sullenly.

The older man sighed. "You shot someone from a distance of more than a kilometer. Only a handful of people in the world could've made that shot. We need you to work for us. Train our snipers and carry out difficult shots. If you sign these documents..." He pulled out some papers from his coat. "...we promise you a much shorter prison sentence. And obviously, citizenship. You'll get to do what you do best, only with the full backing of Norwegian authority."

A long pause. Oleg stared at them with a stone face.

"Is he dead?" said the younger man.

The two men exchanged confused glances.

"We're not really at liberty to say—"

Oleg nodded. "You have to promise to get my wife and daughter here. They are in danger and must be given full protection."

They nodded.

"I'm sure we can arrange that," said the younger man. "Do you have an address?"

The older man took out a blank piece of paper and a pen from his coat. Oleg scribbled down the address and then signed the papers.

"Very well," the older man said. "We look forward to working with you. There will be a trial, but we'll make sure the prosecutor doesn't ask for more than five years. Normally, you'd be looking at least fifteen."

"Can I get that in writing."

The two men smiled.

"I'm sure nobody wants any additional paperwork from this conversation," said the older man. "Least of all, you."

They stood.

"Please sit," said the younger man. "We'll get someone to come pick you up."

Outside the interrogation room, the two happened upon Detective Inspector Dundre.

"Frantzen. Martinsen."

"Dundre."

"What happened? Did you get him to confess?"

"We wouldn't have done our job if we hadn't done that."

The older man gave the confession to Dundre. "Now you can claim the honor and talk to the press, and we'll take care of the prosecution. Look at this as a win-win situation."

The two men lifted their hats and disappeared down the hallway.

———

WHEN FELICIA ENTERED Kurt Hammer's room, he was on the phone.

"Okay, thanks, Frank. I have a visitor here, so I'm going to hang up. Have a nice day." He turned to her. "Good to see that you are alive."

She smiled. "The doctor insisted that I should go lie down. I said I would if he promised to push me to your room."

Erlandsen rolled the bed in beside Kurt and left the room.

"Do you remember what happened?" she asked. "The damn morphine destroyed my short-term memory."

"I held you close to me. I should've asked you to lie on the floor, but you survived, in any case."

She got out of bed, pulling the morphine apparatus along with her, and kissed him on the cheek.

"Thank you. I owe you my life."

PERPETRATOR APPREHENDED

BY FRANK HANSEN

Early yesterday morning, a Russian man, Oleg Abakumov, was detained by police at Trondheim Central Station. He was on his way to Oslo.

Abakumov confessed to the attempted murder of journalist Kurt Hammer and the assault on journalist Felicia Alvdal. Both work for Aftenbladet.

Victory

Detective Inspector Roy Dundre calls the confession and arrest a victory for the Trondheim Police.

"We've had a great deal to investigate in the past month, and there are still many unknown pieces in this puzzle. Therefore, this was a victory for us."

Calm

The interrogation was peaceful," said Dundre. "He had no other weapons other than the one he had abandoned in a dumpster near the Scandic Lerkendal hotel. We found it pretty quickly, and are working to establish that the bullets which were found in Felicia Alvdal's shoulder could have been fired from this weapon."

Amazing

The weapon is a Mosin-Nagant M91/30 PU Sniper rifle. Aftenbladet has talked with weapons expert Find Lium from Tynset, and he is very impressed.

"If the distance you've given me is correct, this is absolutely amazing," said Lium. "There are only a handful of people in the world that can hit a target at a distance of one kilometer. This man must have had special training or be a natural talent."

MARCH 1, 2012

"Are you coming?"

Olya nodded. She took her time pulling the red dress over her head.

A dark-haired lady who said her name was Felicia had brought it for her weeks after the explosion.

"Thank you," Olya had whispered. Kurt?"

"Yeah, I'm a colleague of his. I figured you both needed some new clothes."

Olya now looked at herself in the mirror. It was an old-fashioned dress with lace and white flowers.

"How do I look?"

"Great!" The voice of the blonde policewoman, Line, had a motherly quality that made Olya feel safe.

Outside, it was pouring rain as they got into the police car waiting between the large concrete blocks that constituted St. Olav's Hospital. Olya hobbled toward it and spent a long time getting into the vehicle.

She stared out the window as the car sped up. In spite of the constant rain, she found this city more attractive than

Moscow. Everything here was smaller, more intimate. The clothes, the houses, the number of beggars. At the same time, flashier and more extravagant. Trondheim appeared to her as a miniature Moscow without all the noise and dirt.

INSIDE THE INTERROGATION ROOM, Detective Inspector Roy Dundre sat waiting for Olya with two cups of coffee. She sat on the other side of the wide table.

He pressed a pedal under the table. "Interview with Olya Volkova began on the 1st of March 2012, at 11:15 a.m." He looked at her. "It's good to finally have you here. I suppose Line has already told you that we're placing you under arrest?"

Olya nodded.

"Good. We have evidence that you killed Petter Jansrud and Christian Blekstad." He pulled out some papers and put them on the table. "If you plead guilty, I will do everything I can to make sure you get a reduced sentence."

"It wasn't murder. They assaulted me. It was self-defense."

Dundre snorted. "Do you really expect me to believe that?"

"I don't care what you believe. Have you captured Erik Larsen?"

Dundre looked at her, questioningly.

"He raped me and threatened to murder me."

"Would you be willing two testify?"

"When is the trial?"

Dundre thought for a moment. "I'll let you know. You're going to put this man down for good. In the meantime, you're under arrest." He stood to leave the room, but turned in the doorway. "Oh, and by the way, you're lucky. Line has informed me about the state of your legs, and we've arranged for access to a physician three days a week. Enjoy your stay."

A BLACK MERCEDES rolled into the concrete port labeled *Correctional Services Trondheim Prison.* The inscription was framed by a metal arch embedded in the concrete. The top of the concrete door was also crowned by a strip of metal. Underneath the inscription, a metal garage door was built into the wall and framed by a blue arch.

The Mercedes continued into an oblong red-brick building and halted. Out of the car stepped a man with gray hair, wearing glasses, a plaid shirt, and a gray coat. In his left hand he held a briefcase. In front of the iron doors of the red-brick building, a man stood waiting. He was a head taller than the other and dressed in a suit.

"Is he ready," the man with glasses said to the other.

"He's waiting."

ERIK LARSEN WAS SITTING on the bed, awaiting a visit to his cell, which was small and consisted of a toilet, a desk and chair, a wood cabinet–shelf combo, and a bed. He had put a little TV and stereo on the desk.

Erik could hear a key being inserted on the other side of the blue cell door. A man with gray hair, wearing glasses and a gray coat over a plaid shirt was admitted inside.

"Hello." the man said.

"Hello." Erik gestured toward the chair in front of the desk.

"Thanks." The man sat, stripped his coat, and extended a hand. "Tor Erling Staff. "

"Erik Larsen."

"Let's see." Staff put his briefcase on his lap and removed a stack of papers, then put the case back on the floor.

Erik sat motionless and stared at them.

"You are charged with the premeditated murder of Stieg Homme, and terrorist activities against Trondheim Torg. Do you have any thoughts on how you want to plead?"

"The guy attacked me. It was self-defense."

Staff sighed. "You are aware that with your track record, the court will have trouble believing that?"

"I don't care."

"When it comes to terrorist activities—"

"I am not guilty."

Staff leaned back. "Well, we don't know what evidence they have, but I doubt they would've charged you if they didn't have enough."

"I don't care."

"In other words, you are pleading Not Guilty to all the charges?"

"Correct."

Staff placed the briefcase back on his lap and returned the stack of papers. Then he stood and put on his gray overcoat. Erik Larsen stared at the floor, anxious about getting his freedom back.

Staff moved toward the exit. "One more thing." He turned in the doorway. I got a text from the public prosecutor not long ago. You will be charged with rape and death threats against Olya Volkova. How do you plead?"

MARCH 20, 2012

THE COURTHOUSE IN TRONDHEIM WAS A LARGE, RED granite building. In front of the green door stood a statue of a bearded man in marble who peered beyond the venerable steps that led into the building.

Munkegata Street was chocked full of cars, from the ruins of Trondheim Torg to the Nidaros Cathedral. Police vehicles, private cars, and press vehicles from TV2, CNN, BBC, and Fox News. Like in the trial of Breivik the prior year, only part of the trial was televised, but that didn't make it any less attractive to the media.

As Erik Larsen was led into courtroom 309, with slicked-back hair and wearing a gray Armani suit and handcuffs, Kurt Hammer and Frank Hansen sat on the premier press bench.

"Glad you could join me," Kurt said to Frank.

"I'm not sure I'm allowed to be with you every day, but I convinced Alex that you needed support when you came out of the hospital." Frank chuckled.

A few hundred miles northeast of Trondheim, a passenger plane had just landed at Sheremetyevo airport in Moscow.

"Why us," young Frantzen said to the much older Martinsen, as they waited for a taxi.

"Why not. Someone has pick them up. Be glad you got a paid trip to Moscow.

"Could've gone on just fine without it." Frantzen looked at the gray sky and pulled his gray coat tighter around himself.

Half an hour later, the two stood in the Yogozapadnya neighborhood and looked up at an apartment building which looked to have been built in the mid-fifties.

"Should be here." Martinsen took out a note from his coat pocket and checked it against the faded number plate on the side of the brick building.

They strode toward entrance 14C and rang the bell. The door opened almost immediately.

"Follow me." Martinsen as he proceeded over the doorstep and removed a Colt pistol from inside his coat.

He lifted it with both hands and pointed it ahead as he moved forward. Frantzen wanted to protest, but his instinct told him that now wasn't the time.

They traveled to the eighth floor, and Martinsen slowly turned the doorknob. Inside, there was a narrow aisle beside a woman standing next to a man wearing a black T-shirt, combat boots, military trousers, a military jacket, and a balaclava. He held a Luger P08 against her temple. The woman had shoulder-length, raven-black hair, a round face that shone with terror, full red lips, and big breasts.

"You better have Oleg, or she dies," he said, from underneath the balaclava.

Frantzen and Martinsen exchanged glances. In a split second, Martinsen fired a shot into the man's forehead, and

Frantzen a shot his leg. The man fell to the ground, but not without a shot being fired toward the ceiling. The woman knelt and put her face in her hands.

Frantzen ran over to her and put his coat around her. "Are you Anna?"

"Yes. But they took my baby, Anastasia!"

Martinsen sprinted down the hall. Inside a small room with a double bed and a cot, he noticed that the bottom of the cot was covered by a blanket. He took out a handkerchief lifted the carpet. What he saw was a blue corpse of a baby. He put the blanket back and walked back to his colleague.

"She's dead. There's no point in taking her with us. We must go before the police show up. Here, we're far beyond our jurisdiction."

Frantzen nodded and turned to the woman. "There's nothing more we can do for Anastasia. If you want to say good-bye, she's still in her crib. But make it quick. The police will be arriving at any moment. Your husband is waiting for you in Norway. If you want to see him, you better come with us."

"Has he been arrested?"

"I'll explain on the way. Now's not the time."

The woman turned to the bedroom.

"By the way, use this." Frantzen pulled out a plastic glove from his coat.

She looked at him and pulled it on, reluctantly. Inside the bedroom, she lifted the baby out of the cot and held it close to her for a few seconds.

As sirens approached the block, the three of them hurried downstairs and got into a taxi on the other side of the street.

———

"Can the accused stand up?"

The buzz in courtroom 309 died down when Judge Wenche Arntzen's spoke.

"One indictment has been taken out against Erik Theodor Larsen. According to the decision, you are charged with violating Penal Code section 147a, as provided in paragraphs 148, 151a, 151b, first paragraph, c and f, third paragraph, 152, second paragraph, 152a, first, third, and fourth paragraphs, 152b, 152C, 153, subsections 154, 223 second paragraph, 231c and f, 232, and 233. You are also charged with violating Criminal Code section 192 which deals with a., persons obtaining sexual intercourse by violence or by threatening behavior. Or b., persons obtaining sexual intercourse with someone who is unconscious or otherwise unable to oppose the action. Or c., someone who, by violence or threatening behavior, causes someone to have sexual relations with another, or to perform similar actions with themselves. You are also charged with violating Criminal Code section 233, which deals with whomsoever causes another's death, or who is accessory thereto. Have the accused understood the indictment?"

Erik Larsen glanced at Tor Erling Staff, who nodded.

"Yes, Judge," Erik said.

"Then you will be hereinafter be referred to as *the accused*. Do you acknowledge culpability?"

"No."

"Then you may be seated."

Olya entered courtroom 309, handcuffed. She sat on a chair in front of the golden wood podium in the middle of the room, where the big police officer who had brought her into the room unlocked the handcuffs. The walls were covered from the middle down with golden wooden paneling, and from the middle up in white lime. One long wall behind Erik Larsen and Tor Erling Staff was adorned with two paintings of abstract art in bright colors.

"You are called as a witness in this matter," said Judge Arntzen. "Are you aware that it may lead to prosecution if you do not answer truthfully?"

"Yes," Olya replied.

"Good. Repeat after me. I promise to tell the whole truth, on my honor and conscience."

Olya put her right hand over her chest and repeated the sentence.

"In your statement to the police, you have said that you came to Norway to get a better life, and ended up making a living as a prostitute. Is this true?"

"Yes, that is correct."

"Can you explain how you came into contact with Mr. Larsen?"

"He was my client. He found me online."

"The next thing I want to ask about is difficult, but I have to. In his statement to the police, Larsen claimed that you tried to kill him. Can you explain what happened."

"He called me a whore and held a knife to my throat, which I turned toward him and pressed against his neck."

A gasp went through the hall.

Olya didn't blink. "I could have killed him then and there, but I decided to throw the knife on the floor."

"And then you were taken to Trolla Brug, correct?"

"That's right. I think my strength frightened him, so he threw me away and got out of bed to pick up a gun from his pants on the floor and point it at me. Then he told me that I should get out of bed and put on my clothes. I did as he said, and then he drove me to Trolla, on his motorbike."

"Did you at any time attempt to escape?"

"He beat me unconscious with his pistol, and when I regained consciousness, I was in Trolla."

"Please describe what happened."

"They discussed whether they would kill me."

"They?"

"Members of Hell's Angels, I think. All of them were motorcyclists. I was desperate, so I offered them..." Olya turned.

She searched the room and found Kurt on the premier press bench. He looked exactly as he had the first time she saw him, as a scruffy version of Jeff Bridges, in a canary yellow suit and a fedora, but now with a broken arm. Her gaze met his, and she hoped that he could read *sorry* from her eyes.

"... Kurt Hammer."

"Were they looking for him?"

"Yes. Apparently, they felt he was responsible for the death of their brothers. Despite his violent nature and temper, Erik Larsen isn't a fool. He realized that I could be useful, so they threw me into a dark room and locked the door. After a few hours, they came back and drove their bikes inside. Then not long afterward, I could hear sirens outside. I thought everyone had been taken by the police. But they hadn't, because on what must've been the next day, Erik came back and drove me to a hotel in town."

"Again, did you at any time try to escape."

"No. I was too weak and hungry. Erik got me into a room at the hotel. I think he knew the guy at the front desk. And he told me that I should send a message to Kurt. I did so and then went to sleep. When I woke up, Kurt was in the room. I wanted to tell him everything, but he confronted me, and then..."

"What happened?"

"There was an explosion, and I knew right away."

"What did you know?"

"That Erik was behind it. There was no doubt in my mind."

THE DARK SIDE OF PROSTITUTION

BY KURT HAMMER AND FRANK HANSEN

Approximately fifteen hundred women are offering sexual services in Norway via ads. One of those women was Olya Volkova.

Volkova was born in Moscow, to a Russian father and half-Spanish mother. Like so many others in Russia after the fall of the wall, her father lost his job and began to spend more and more time at the local watering hole. Volkova had to grow up with an alcoholic father who beat and abused her mother, ultimately resulting in her mother's untimely death. Once her mother was no longer present, there was no one standing between Volkova and her father.

The evening after the funeral, he had been drinking heavily, and decided to take out his frustration and sadness on his only daughter. An ordinary young woman would have resigned after being forced to experience so many years of psychological terror. But Volkova defended herself and ended up killing her father in self-defense.

Because of Russia's widespread culture of corruption, and because there were no witnesses to what had taken place,

Volkova didn't see any other option but to flee to another country.

No Opportunities

Because the family had been forced to live on her mother's disability benefits, Olya was financially broke when she passed. But several years in a caring role for the mother who really should have taken care of her, led to Volkova's survival instinct being sharpened.

What does a young woman without future prospects do when she has no post-secondary education, and is forced to leave her country?" For Volkova, the choice was easy. Sell her body, or risk a future in prison or a mental hospital.

As luck would have it, an old acquaintance of her father—a shop owner near the family's apartment—was interested in her and had enough money to realize her desperate plan. Barely a day after she had to make a fateful choice to avoid persecution, she was sitting on a flight to one of the world's richest countries.

No Welcoming Committee

When she landed at Værnes airport, Volkova was as poor as she'd been right after her mother died. What met her in Norway was a cold Scandinavian reality check. The first man she tried to sell herself to, lawyer Christian Blekstad, proved to be a dangerous man. He yelled at her and beat her nearly unconscious, whereupon she drowned him. She claims this was partly from fear, partly because her survival instinct took over, and partly in self-defense.

Rapist

Christian Blekstad has raped a woman at least once before. A source that Aftenbladet has spoken to, said the case was hushed when she tried to report him to the management at her workplace. When she finally couldn't got to work anymore, she was fired.

The source's doctor, Martine Skog, is working as general practitioner at Gildheim Medical Center. She adds that her patient received lifelong injuries resulting from the rape.

"Absolutely horrible case. I encouraged her to go to the police, but she believed there was no point. In a way, I understand her. The injuries she suffered are extensive and include damage to the anal sphincter muscles, destruction of nerves in the bowel tract, and bacterial infection that may have led to cancer."

The CEO of *Adnor Lawyers*, Hans Løten, is tight-lipped regarding the allegations.

"We encouraged her to go to the police. If this was perceived that her case was hushed, it is highly regrettable. Unfortunately, we can't do anything against an employee on the basis of allegations coming from another employee. It wouldn't be fair."

Trondheim Police Press Contact, Anne K. Hope, confirmed that no report was received from Aftenbladet's source.

"Unfortunately, we don't have the resources to follow up all rape reports coming in. In practice, we only deal with a few percent, and very few of them end up in the criminal justice system, as it is difficult to gather evidence in the aftermath of an incident."

A Nightmare

From there, Volkova's story only worsens. On the 28th of January, she was contacted by known cross-country skier Petter Jansrud. She agreed to go to his house in Byåsen the next day. What began as an ordinary transaction evolved into a nightmare.

Jansrud drugged her and carried her into his bedroom. But the dosage was incorrect. After he had gone down to the kitchen to consume alcohol, Volkova woke up. When he came back with a knife, allegedly to kill her, a scuffle developed, which Volkova eventually won.

When the undersigned arrived at the scene a few hours later, the body of Jansrud was hung with ropes, between the walls of the living room, with his own penis shoved into his mouth. Volkova had escaped another sadistic rapist. This time, with her life barely intact.

Aftenbladet has been in contact with a source who was close to Jansrud. She had experienced a new side of him one stormy night, when he came to her home. He ended up hitting her and breaking her nose, after which he tied her to the bed and raped her in the most gruesome way. The case was reported but later dropped.

Trondheim Police Press Contact, Hope, is aware of the case and regrettably acknowledges that it was dropped.

"Here, we had evidence in the form of a written medical certificate and radiographs. But the case was unfortunately dismissed because of insufficient evidence when it wasn't possible to link the damage to Jansrud."

Kᴜʀᴛ Hᴀᴍᴍᴇʀ ᴛᴏ ʜɪs ᴘʜᴏɴᴇ ʀɪɴɢɪɴɢ ᴏɴ ᴛʜᴇ nightstand. It was 1:15 a.m.

He groggily picked up the phone. "Hammer."

"Hi, this is Magne Lundvoll, Olya's Defender. Sorry I'm calling so late, but I've been up preparing for the case."

"Is it about Olya?"

"Yes. I read your story in Aftenbladet. It turns the entire trial on its head. I will use it as evidence, unless..."

"What?"

"... you can persuade your sources to stand as witnesses."

"I'll see what I can do."

"Thank you. This will really help Olya."

Kurt Hammer lay down to sleep again, with a satisfied smile.

He woke up with a splitting headache. *What had happened last night? Of course. Anne Berit and Rachel!*

He had barely gotten out of the double bed, when the phone rang. It was Editor Karlsen.

"Kurt!"

"Boss. What's happening?"

"I need you to join Frank at a news conference at police headquarters, in a couple hours. They're going to deliver Erik Larsen's verdict."

"You know, I got asked last night to obtain testimony for Olya."

"This'll only take a couple hours."

Kurt sighed. "All right, I'll do it."

He hung up, took his canary yellow suit into the bathroom and discovered a nearly empty Jack Daniels bottle on the sink, under the mirror.

"Note to self—drink less." He got into the shower.

On the bus on the way to the police station, he cursed that it was almost full, and reminded himself that he had to get money from the insurance company for his blown-up motorcycle. Yet he couldn't help but smile when he got a message from Felicia, who was still hospitalized.

Thinking of you – F.

Inside the police station, the atmosphere was mixed. Most journalists agreed that the police had done a good job with the trial, but concern for another attack of a similar nature was as oppressive as the rain splashing against the large glass facades.

Detective Inspector Dundre was in unusually good spirits as he took to the makeshift bench that had been set up at the entrance of the office space. He came along with Police Chief Voll, who for the occasion wore his white police hat with a black brim and a gold emblem on the front. Both oozed pride.

"As you know," said Voll, "we have ensured that the man behind the horrible and cowardly attack on Trondheim Torg has been incarcerated for the foreseeable future. Head of the investigation was Roy Dundre, sitting on my right, and he deserves all possible praise for the great police work. He has also collaborated with, amongst others, Criminal Inspector

Harry Olsen, on my left. They will now answer questions. Thank you."

Kurt was the first to rise, while Frank took pictures.

"How is the protective and security assessment in Trondheim right now? Can the audience feel safe?"

Roy Dundre leaned forward to the microphone. "We have worked closely with NCIS during the investigation, and they've said that the terrorist threat is small in Trondheim right now. They are obviously regretting that they didn't see this attack coming."

———

A COUPLE HOURS LATER, Frank and Kurt were sitting in Frank's Volkswagen Passat. Frank backed out from the chaos of cars from TV2, NRK, CNN, BBC and other news outlets.

"Got a couple hours to kill?" Kurt asked.

"Not really. I have to go home and help with dinner before I edit pictures."

"I got a call yesterday from Olya's lawyer. He wanted me to help get Anne Berit's and Rachel's testimonies."

Frank sighed and took his phone out of his coat pocket.

"What're you doing?" Kurt said.

"Calling home and asking for permission." The phone rang a few times, then, "Hello, dear. I have to help Kurt persuade the victims from the story to give their testimonies." He sounded as if he was begging, but that wasn't his intention. "Yes, I'll try to be quick. Love you."

"How did it go?"

"She wasn't happy. But she respects what I'm doing."

Ten minutes later, Frank parked outside Øvre Møllenberg 41. The rain slammed so hard on the window panes that both took off their overcoats inside the car and held them over their heads while they ran to the door.

Rachel opened almost immediately. "Come in, come in. What terrible weather."

When they got inside, Rachel extended a hand to Kurt.

"I'm assuming you're Kurt? Good to finally get to meet you!"

"Likewise."

"What are you doing here?" Rachel asked.

"I ..."

"Kurt," said Frank.

They exchanged glances filled with uncertainty and embarrassment.

"Maybe we could have a cup of coffee," Frank said.

"Of course. Come in."

Rachel helped Kurt hang up his gray jacket, and then all three of them went into the living room with an open kitchen solution. Rachel made coffee and sat on the other side of the table.

"I think Kurt should explain why we're here," said Frank.

"I got a phone call yesterday from Olya's lawyer. She needs help. It isn't certain that she'll avoid jail, but to make sure she gets as low of a sentence as possible, the jury must be convinced that she killed in self-defense. Or at least felt threatened. And that's where..." He looked at Frank.

"You come in," said Frank.

"You want me to testify," Rachel whispered.

"You're protected under journalistic source protection, of course," Kurt said. "But Olya needs you."

Rachel sighed. "All right. I'll do it if that lawyer can promise me that I'll get to testify without being discussed in the media."

"I believe that the case will proceed at least partially behind closed doors," said Kurt. "I'll have him call you."

———

As they drove towards Gardermoens Street, where Anne Berit's apartment was located, Kurt said, "She's pleased with me now, you now."

Frank looked at him. "Who?"

"Marte. She's smiling at me from up there, somewhere. Alex should be happy with you, too."

Frank smiled. "She is. She's just frustrated. I understand her, in some ways. It bothers her that she can't find a job. But I hope it changes."

———

"I have to think about it," Anne Berit said. "There's a reason I'm living on disability pension."

The rain pounded on the window panes of the old apartment which smelled of Friele coffee and Earl Grey tea.

"I think you can give your testimony at the police station if you aren't comfortable with standing up in court," Frank said, in a soothing voice.

"Here's the number to the lawyer," Kurt said. "You can call after you've thought about it," He handed the middle-aged woman a handwritten note.

She pulled her glasses up on her nose and looked at it. "That, I will do. But I can't promise anything."

The two men braved the rain once again and hopped into Frank's car.

"Looks like Olya's trial lies in Anne Berit's hands," Kurt said. "Let's hope she does the right thing."

APRIL 29, 2012

Olya's lawsuit was getting just as much attention as Erik Larsen's case. In just a few days, she had gone from being described as a cold-blooded murderer to a victim.

After Kurt and Frank's story came out, interview requests piled up. But the main character herself sat silently in her cell. Commentators from Norway, Iran, the United States, Germany, Scotland, and Egypt wondered if she would be acquitted, and Russia threatened political sanctions if she weren't.

The whole square around the statue of Olav Tryggvason and all of Munkegata Street up to Nidaros Cathedral was full of cars during the last day of trial, when the jury would read the verdict. Kurt Hammer and Frank Hansen had acquired seats on the first press bench, in a room that was completely full.

As Olya was led into the courtroom, in handcuffs, wearing a red floor-length dress and high heels, the entire hall was bathed in flashing camera lights. She kept her head up and didn't smile. Kurt thought she looked like a Spanish samba dancer.

———

OLEG ABAKUMOV LOOKED into his wife's eyes for the first time since he had left Russia.

"How long will you be here," she asked.

"They said they'll try to get me out as soon as possible. I've got a job, Anna. Anastasia will have a safe future!"

Anna put her head in her hands, in the gray visiting room at Leira Prison.

"What is it, vozlyublennyy?"

"They... they took her. She's dead." Anna sobbed.

———

"THE COURT IS SET," Judge Fredriksen announced.

"Honorable Judge, the defense will now introduce the first of two witnesses today. Anne Berit Knutsen."

Anne Berit slowly stood and walked to the witness stand in the middle of the oblong courtroom. She had on a floor-length black dress and her hair was in a bun. She was extremely thin, so much so that Kurt feared she could be perceived by the jury as having an eating disorder.

"Repeat after me, said Judge Fredriksen. I promise to tell the whole truth, on my honor and conscience."

Anne Berit looked at the judge with wide eyes, put her hand on her left breast, and repeated the sentence.

"First," said Olya's Defender, Magne Lundvoll, "can you explain to the court how you knew the deceased, Christian Blekstad?"

"He was a lawyer, employed by my company, Adnor Lawyers," Anne replied. "I worked there as a secretary."

"So your relationship was entirely professional?"

"That's right. Until he... one day ..." She had tears in her eyes. "He asked me into his office to transcribe a letter. But when I came, in he locked the door and grabbed me around my neck. He pressed me against the wall so hard I thought I was going to choke. Then he raped me, anally."

Magne continued, gently. "Did you scream?"

"Yes. Yes, I screamed and made a racket. But we were the only ones in the office at that time."

"When did this happen?"

"Almost exactly one year ago. On the 27th of last April. After the episode, I had lifelong damages, and I had bigger and bigger issues with getting to work. I reported it to the management, but the episode was just shushed down. In the end, I was dismissed because I couldn't manage to come to work anymore and risk seeing Blekstad."

"Do you have any proof of what happened?"

"Nothing except the statement from my doctor, which is referenced in the article by Hammer and Hansen."

Magne leaned back.

"The defense has no further questions."

"Does the prosecution have any questions?" Judge Fredriksen said.

The prosecutor shook his head. Magne Lundvoll coughed. He pushed his black designer glasses further up on his aquiline nose and straightened some of his light brown fringe.

"Now, we were really supposed to present witness number two here," said Lundvoll, "but she hasn't yet arrived. The defense asks for a thirty-minute break to locate her."

"That is approved." Judge Fredriksen slammed the gavel.

During the break, Lundvoll, and eventually Kurt Hammer, tried calling and sending messages to Rachel Skavlan a dozen times, but she didn't answer or respond to the texts.

Once the half-hour was over, rumors began spreading

throughout the audience, especially among journalists, that Rachel wasn't going to show.

"The court is set," announced Judge Fredriksen.

His white hair looked disheveled, and he had a spot of jam in his mustache.

"Has the witness arrived," he asked Magne Lundvoll.

"Unfortunately, Honorable Judge, she—"

The doors opened and in came a middle-aged policeman. He spotted Lundvoll and ran up to him. Everyone in the court-room started whispering.

Lundvoll and the policeman whispered together for a good while.

Then, "Rachel Skavlan made statements to the police, and I've just been handed the recording. Unless the judge has no objection, I will present this as evidence to the court."

Judge Fredriksen scratched his chin. "Well, this is unortho-dox, Lundvoll. Had the prosecution prepared some questions?"

The prosecutor shook his head.

"Well, then I approve it."

After the recording was played, Judge Fredriksen hit the gavel. "The court will recess for two hours to consider the new evidence that has emerged.

———

AFTER TWO HOURS, the court was sat back in motion.

"The court will now request the final statement from the defense," said Judge Fredriksen.

Magne Lundvoll rose. "Distinguished jury, you've read and heard Olya's explanation about how she has protected herself against men that, by victims, have been described as monsters and abusers. Unfortunately, the way in which Volkova reacted is being portrayed as a cold-blooded murderer. But think, honorable jury. Put yourselves in her shoes. How would you have reacted in the same situation? Naturally, she should have gone to the police. But this is a woman who was fleeing, with legitimate reasons to not trust anyone. With this in mind, as well as that she is a foreigner without a thorough knowledge of Norwegian judiciary or executive authorities, not to mention that the assault case of one of the witnesses who testified was dismissed in spite of evidence, means that the defense is forced to ask for a full acquittal on all counts."

Likewise, the court will request the final statement from the prosecution," said Judge Fredriksen.

Prosecutor Harald Stang stood. "Distinguished jury, you have heard the defense characterize Volkova's reaction pattern as depicting her as a cold-blooded murderer. So why shouldn't you believe she is just that? A cold-blooded murderer. According to defense, you shouldn't because of statements from two witnesses. One got her case dismissed, and the other didn't even report her incident to the police. In the story written by journalists Kurt Hammer and Frank Hansen, Volkova has admitted to having killed her father. In this case, we have only her word that this also didn't happen in cold blood. All things considered, the prosecution asks that the accused is found guilty of all charges."

SENTENCE DELIVERED

BY KURT HAMMER, HANNE ESTENSTAD, AND FRANK
HANSEN

Olya Volkova was sentenced yesterday to seven years of imprisonment, with the possibility of parole. She was convicted of
killing two men, but the jury found it probable that she felt
threatened. This was seen as an extenuating circumstance.
Volkova seemed happy with the verdict, and gives thanks, in
part, to Aftenbladet's journalists.
"I want to thank Kurt Hammer and Frank Hansen for their
efforts in telling my story. And I also want to thank my lawyer,
Magne Lundvoll," she told the press, yesterday.
Prosecutor Harald Stang is dissatisfied with the result, but
doesn't think it is sensational.
"My colleague Magne Lundvoll gave a remarkable effort, and
considering the witness statements which were delivered on
the trial's last day, the verdict isn't surprising. But I'm still
disappointed, obviously. My thoughts right now go primarily to
Jansrud's and Blekstad's families, who had a rough experience
yesterday.

Monster

The trial lasted for two weeks and one day, and during that time, family members not only had to listen to Olya's statement, in which she described how she killed the men, but they also had to deal with witness statements from alleged victims of the deceased.

In his closing procedure, Lundvoll referenced one of the statements from a witness where Jansrud was referred to as a monster and a predator. Several of the family members present responded to this with tears and dismay.

Understanding

Defender Magne Lundvoll understands that the trial has been difficult for the relatives.

"Of course it's difficult, and I have full understanding. But these are things that must be carried out for a society to function properly. At the same time, this is a special case, because Olya was both victim and perpetrator at the same time.

EPILOGUE

Kᴜʀᴛ Hᴀᴍᴍᴇʀ ᴡᴀs ᴀᴡᴀᴋᴇɴᴇᴅ ᴡʜᴇɴ ʜɪs ᴘʜᴏɴᴇ ʀᴀɴɢ, on the nightstand. He opened his eyes and realized that the clock was 10:40 a.m.

"Hey, sleepyhead. I'm standing outside."

"Sure, be right there. Couldn't get to sleep last night."

He dragged himself out of bed and threw on canary yellow suit pants and a white shirt. Then he put on the yellow suit jacket before he went out in the hall and opened the front door.

Felicia didn't look like a woman who'd just been discharged from hospital, with her long dark brown hair blowing in the wind. She wore a tight black leather jacket and aviator sunglasses.

"Hey!" She kissed him. "Good to see you again."

"You, too. Is your shoulder bandaged?"

"Yes, it is. But I can bend it, although it still hurts a bit."

They got into her white Mini Cooper.

"I heard rumors that you used to be married." She sped towards the city center.

"Yes. The paperwork was approved. It's the pro forma, of course, but..."

"Congratulations." She smiled at him. "You've done a good thing."

"Yes, Olya said she didn't want to be sent out of the country. Now she can establish herself here."

When they stopped outside Nidaros Cathedral, it started to rain.

"Would you like me to accompany you?" asked Felicia.

"Certainly." He got out of the car, with two flower bouquets.

After searching the cemetery for a while, he found Lise's grave. It was overflowing with flowers, and two pigeons sat on the marble headstone.

"I should've saved her," Kurt said.

"It wasn't your fault." Felicia gripped his hand.

"I was still hospitalized when she was buried, so I didn't have the chance to say goodbye."

"So do it now."

He bent down and put one of the white rose bouquets on top of the pile of lilies and red roses. It looked like a wreath of white sapphires, in the rain.

Finally, they went to Martes grave.

"You know," Kurt whispered.

"What?"

"She's the one who gave me the strength to help Olya. I also think it was her who helped me back to life in the hospital."

He kissed the remaining bouquet and laid it on the grave, next to the last one he had put there.

They stood in the rain for five minutes, in silence, before they went back to the car. On the way to Saupstadflata 3D, Kurt's phone vibrated in his pants pocket.

"Hey, Kurt, it's Frank."

"Hey. What's up?"

"I just wanted to say that Oleg will be sentenced today, in case you would want to be there."

"Oh, no, I'm busy. But I'll let Felicia know. Thanks."

"No problem. Talk to you later."

———

AT HOME, in Eirik Jarl gate 16, Frank stuck his phone in his pocket and straightened his posture. In the living room, Alexandra was sitting on the couch, nursing. Frank walked in and sat beside her.

"Wanna join me outside afterwards?" she said. "I plan to try out the new stroller."

"Okay." He smiled. "Babe, I got a call from the editor today. I've been offered a full-time position."

———

INSIDE COURTROOM 302, in Trondheim Courthouse, Anna was listening to her Russian translator explain Oleg's sentence.

"They say that he's going to get seven years, with the possibility of parole."

Anna smiled for the first time in a long time. In Russia, he would've surely received a lifetime sentence.

———

FELICIA STOPPED her Mini Cooper outside Kolstadflata 3D, which turned out to be a medium-sized red house with white trimmings. It had a huge lawn and was surrounded by trees A small garage was attached.

"Good luck," said Felicia.

"Thanks," Kurt said. "I'll need it."

He stepped out of the car and strode up the paved road, to the house. Inside the living room, a large group of men between thirty and forty years old were seated around an oblong wooden table. Some sat on a brown sofa, others in square wooden chairs. The floor consisted of old wooden planks, and the table was on a red shaggy rug.

Kurt hesitated before he sat in a vacant chair.

"Hey, I'm Kurt Hammer.

"Hey, Kurt Hammer," the others replied.

"And I'm an alcoholic."

THE AUTHOR WISHES TO THANK

Hege Marie Vikaune at the Trondheim Police, for letting me come over to do research.

And Ida Elise Østberg, for positive and prompt feedback on the manuscript. Ashley Conner for wonderful editing, as well as Miika Hannila and the Next Chapter team.

Dear reader,

We hope you enjoyed reading *Trouble In Trondheim*. Please take a moment to leave a review in Amazon, even if it's a short one. Your opinion is important to us.

The story continues in Murder In Lima.

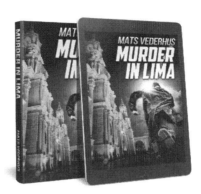

Discover more books by Mats Vederhus at https://www. nextchapter.pub/authors/mats-vederhus

Want to know when one of our books is free or discounted for Kindle? Join the newsletter at http://eepurl.com/bqqB3H

Best regards,
Mats Vederhus and the Next Chapter Team

Printed in Great Britain
by Amazon